A Chick Thing

Book
2

Grosset & Dunlap

A Chick Thing

Book 2

By Daniella Burr

Based on a teleplay
written by Doug Tuber and Tim Maile

A Stan Rogow Book • Grosset & Dunlap

GROSSET & DUNLAP
Published by the Penguin Group
Penguin Group (USA) Inc., 375 Hudson Street, New York, New York 10014, U.S.A.
Penguin Group (Canada), 10 Alcorn Avenue, Toronto, Ontario, Canada M4V 3B2
(a division of Pearson Penguin Canada Inc.)
Penguin Books Ltd, 80 Strand, London WC2R 0RL, England
Penguin Ireland, 25 St Stephen's Green, Dublin 2, Ireland
(a division of Penguin Books Ltd)
Penguin Group (Australia), 250 Camberwell Road, Camberwell, Victoria 3124,
Australia (a division of Pearson Australia Group Pty Ltd)
Penguin Books India Pvt Ltd, 11 Community Centre, Panchsheel Park,
New Delhi - 110 017, India
Penguin Group (NZ), Cnr Airborne and Rosedale Roads, Albany, Auckland 1310,
New Zealand (a division of Pearson New Zealand Ltd)
Penguin Books (South Africa) (Pty) Ltd, 24 Sturdee Avenue, Rosebank, Johannesburg
2196, South Africa

Penguin Books Ltd, Registered Offices:
80 Strand, London WC2R 0RL, England

Text copyright © 2005 Stan Rogow Productions (U.S.),
© 2005 Temple Street Releasing Limited (Canada).
Series and logo copyright © 2005 Darcy Productions Limited,
a subsidiary of Temple Street Productions Limited.
DISCOVERY KIDS, DISCOVERY and all related indicia are
trademarks of Discovery Communications, Inc., used under license.
All rights reserved. DiscoveryKids.com

Published by Grosset & Dunlap, a division of Penguin Young Readers Group,
345 Hudson Street, New York, New York 10014.
GROSSET & DUNLAP is a trademark of Penguin Group (USA) Inc.
Printed in the U.S.A.

Library of Congress Control Number: 2005011439

ISBN 0-448-43988-3   10 9 8 7 6 5 4 3 2 1

Hi!

I'm Sara, and I play Darcy Fields on <u>Darcy's Wild Life</u>. I'm so excited to be writing to you!

On <u>Darcy's Wild Life</u>, Darcy is the daughter of a movie star, accustomed to premieres, private jets, and partying in style—so, it was quite a shock when her mother decided to leave such a glamorous life for a "normal life" on a farm in the middle of nowhere.

I love Darcy because she is an optimist and so am I. In real life my childhood has been the opposite of Darcy's. I grew up in California with two great parents, and I have only one animal in my home, my pet dog, Jenny.

I've always wanted to be an actress, and it's amazing to see my dreams coming true. In some ways my life may be easier than Darcy's, but the point is that for better or worse, we all find ourselves in situations that are totally unfamiliar or unexpected. Darcy complains, sure, but at heart, she really does her best to get with the program—and she learns a lot about herself in the process. Personally, I think that's a great lesson!

I hope you enjoy my books, and thank you for watching my show.

Best Wishes!

♡ always,

Sara Paxton

❋ (DARCY'S DISH) ❋

Hey, my people!
Greetings from Farm Country!

You know, I've been gone from Malibu for a couple of weeks
now, and I just can't get used to living out here. Life in a small
farm town is just so different than anything back home.

I have got to stop saying that. Malibu isn't home anymore.
Bailey is. Which means instead of Pilates classes and manicures,
I'm spending my days working at the local animal clinic and
doing—you're not going to believe this—chores!

Of course, some things remain the same no matter where you
go. Even here in Bailey, there are chick problems and guy
problems. In my case, the chick problems include getting my
new pal Lindsay to break out of her uptight, organized shell. As
for the guy problems, well, my main problem is I don't have
one at the moment.

But I'm still looking. I'll keep you posted if the man of my
dreams does show up.

Darcy

Chapter 1

Wild Wisdom . . . *Hawks have the best eyesight in the entire animal world—they can see greater distances and eight times clearer than humans can.*

"Hey, Mom!" Darcy Fields called out as she stepped onto her front porch. She shielded her eyes against the early morning sun and scanned the ranch for her mother. Darcy found her leaning against a ladder that had been propped up against a tree near the side of their ranch house. It was obvious that Victoria Fields was working on some sort of farm-related project, as she often did these days, but Darcy had no idea what this chore was.

She didn't particularly care, either. At the moment, the beautiful blond teen was far more interested in an article she had just discovered in the latest issue of *Star Talk* magazine than anything that was happening in the town of Bailey.

These days, Darcy always seemed to have her head

buried in some sort of celebrity mag. She loved reading about the lives of California's rich and famous—the parties, the beaches, the fashions, and all the newest hot spots. Although, reading about the high life was sort of bittersweet. The articles reminded her of her home in Malibu.

The only problem was, Malibu wasn't actually Darcy's home anymore. Her mother, the famous British actress Victoria Fields, had picked up and moved—taking Darcy with her—far from all of the excitement and glamour of Tinseltown, the center of celebrity. She'd dropped her here in the town of Bailey, which was the center of . . . well . . . *nothing*, actually.

At the moment, being stuck here in Bailey was the source of a huge problem for Darcy. The thing she wanted most in life—at least this week—was to be back in Malibu. And somehow, she had to convince her mother to let her go back there, just for this one weekend.

"You know how I said I'd clean out the hayloft Saturday?" the teen asked, giving her mother her very best *aren't-I-so-adorable-you-just-can't-say-no* look. "Instead of that, can I fly to Malibu for the night?"

Victoria glanced at her daughter. "Do you have the money for airfare, a hotel, and a taxi?" she asked.

Darcy was shocked. She couldn't believe what her mother was asking of her. "A taxi?" she repeated, stunned. "Excuse me, a *limo*."

Victoria chuckled. "I'm sorry. Do you have money for a limo?" she corrected herself.

"No." Darcy shook her head and frowned. "I don't even have money for the tip for a *limo*."

Victoria shrugged. "You know the new rules. . . ." she reminded her.

That was the kiss of death. "I know, I know. If I want something, I have to earn it myself," Darcy said as she let out a heavy sigh. There was no way with the puny pay from her part-time job at the Creature Comforts animal clinic she was going to be able to come up with that kind of cash before Saturday. Especially since she hadn't exactly been saving her paychecks up until now. Somehow, Darcy never seemed to have money when she needed it. After all, even out here in the middle of nowhere it was possible to buy clothing and makeup. The Internet was a dangerous thing! "I don't know where you came up with that rule," Darcy continued, "but it's almost as crazy as moving us to the middle of nowhere to begin with."

Victoria smiled brightly. "Of course it's crazy. I'm an eccentric actress," she said playfully. She noticed the magazine in Darcy's hands and smiled slightly. Suddenly the whole conversation began to make sense. Obviously, the press had gotten word of a party to be given by a member of Darcy's old crowd. (*More likely they'd been sent a press release about it, since that was what the entertainment crowd tended to do,* she thought ruefully.) "What's up in Malibu on Saturday?" she asked her daughter.

"My friend Sienna Clark's birthday party," Darcy explained, pointing to the page in the magazine that revealed the information. "Her dad's having his record company get Cirque du Soleil to perform on his beach in front of their house. I'm pretty sure Sienna would want me there." Darcy looked hopefully at her mother and used her most pitiful voice, all in the hopes that Victoria would bend—just this once— and give Darcy the money she needed to make it to the party.

Unfortunately, Victoria wasn't that easily persuaded. "I'm sorry, sweetie," she replied.

Darcy frowned but said nothing. The thought of missing the amazing circus performance at Sienna's party was absolutely painful.

"You know what I used to do when I didn't get something I really wanted?" Victoria asked, hoping to smooth things over a bit. "I'd pretend it was really stupid and anybody who wanted it was a big loser."

That sounded logical. "Hey, yeah!" Darcy exclaimed. She stood there for a minute, trying desperately to believe that she didn't want to be anywhere near Sienna's fabulous party, with its French-Canadian circus performers, gorgeous Malibu beachfront locale, exotic catered food, and outrageously expensive goody bags.

But it was no use. "Nope, didn't work," she said finally.

Victoria shrugged. "Well, you may be missing catered sushi and clowns on the beach, but here you can see the wonders of nature! Like eggs!" Her eyes nearly danced with excitement.

"Uh-huh . . ." Darcy looked at her mother peculiarly. *Where does she come up with these things?* "Do they have hollandaise sauce on them?" she asked, confused.

Victoria shook her head and gazed up toward the top of the tree. "Could you explain, Eli?"

Darcy followed her mother's eyes and discovered that Eli, a local kid whom Victoria had hired as a ranch hand/local flora-and-fauna expert, was standing at the top of the ladder. His arms were extended straight out as he attempted to reach up in between the highest branches of the tree. Darcy frowned slightly. The top rung of a ladder was not exactly the best place for a kid like Eli. He was kind of accident-prone.

But Eli didn't seem the least bit bothered by his precarious perch. He was far too intent on what he was doing to worry about his own safety. "They're hawk's eggs," he explained to Darcy. "Environmental poisons like pesticides are making their eggshells too thin."

"Eli can't make pancakes to save his life, and don't leave him alone with a leaf rake," Victoria joked, her blue eyes dancing. "But it turns out he knows an astonishing amount about animals."

"We're taking the eggs out of the nest and replacing them with fake ones," Eli explained to Darcy. "That way the weak shells won't get crushed by the momma bird."

Darcy watched the excitement on Eli's face as he explained the plight of the hawks. His eyes grew wide and his shoulder-length brown hair moved around his face as his head bobbed up and down slightly. Eli was kind of cute, in a country boy kind of way. Not that she would ever think of him in *that* way. More importantly, he was apparently pretty smart in the creature department. "Wow, check out nature boy," Darcy remarked, obviously impressed.

"The mother hawk will think she's sitting on her eggs," Victoria continued the explanation, "while we're hatching them in an incubator. Then we'll put the babies back in the nest, and she'll think she hatched them. Easy as one, two, three."

Darcy sighed. It sounded like a good plan. Unfortunately, when Eli was around, even the best plans ran into trouble. . . .

"Okay, got 'em!" Eli announced as he gingerly took the hawk nest in his hands. He took a step down onto the next rung of the ladder. Unfortunately, he must have missed a rung because suddenly, the ladder slipped away from the tree. "Uh oh!" Eli shouted out as the ladder tilted backward, carrying him with it. "Aw no!"

Bam! The ladder hit the ground, and Eli landed flat on the pieces of the rungs. The pain was excruciating. "Ooooo," he moaned.

"Oh my heavens!" Victoria exclaimed. Her concern was clear from the look on her face.

"It's okay," Eli assured her. "I'm all right."

"No, no, no," Victoria replied, shaking her head. "Are the *eggs* okay?"

Eli held up the nest to give her a better view. "They're fine," he told her. "I think I might've sprained my shoulder. . . ."

"But the eggs are okay?" Victoria asked again.

Darcy reached down and gingerly took the eggs from the nest and began to examine them closely.

"One of my feet is kinda numb, too," Eli continued.

But Darcy and Victoria were focused completely on the hawk eggs. "They're fine, Mom, look . . ." Darcy reassured her frantic mother.

Victoria carefully scrutinized each of the pale, bluish-white eggs. They all seemed to be in perfect condition. "Thank goodness," she sighed as she and Darcy started off toward the house, eggs in hand. "We'll get them in an incubator and everything should be fine."

Well, *almost* everything, anyway. Eli was still lying there on the ground, alone, forgotten, and in quite a bit of pain.

"So I think I'll lie here awhile, then. Look at the clouds," he called out even though there was no one left to hear him. He glanced up at the sky. "Hey, that cloud looks like a camel," he mused, just as a sharp pain hit him in the shoulder. "Ow!"

Chapter 2

Wild Wisdom . . . *Oysters filter about fifty gallons of water a day.*

Victoria may have been satisfied spending her days waiting for baby hawks to emerge from their eggs, but Darcy still longed for her old life in the fast lane. Try as she might, she simply couldn't get Sienna's party out of her mind. The thought that all her California friends would be partying without her was excruciatingly frustrating.

If she were in California right now, Darcy would most certainly be busy shopping on exclusive Rodeo Drive, coming up with the perfect outfit for a circus-themed beach party. Maybe a zebra-print bikini? Or perhaps a tiger print instead?

But there was no point in even thinking about it, really. After all, she wasn't getting to Malibu this weekend. Instead of shopping she was stuck at

Creature Comforts, counting the animal clinic's packages of diarrhea pills and stacking flea collars behind the counter.

To Darcy's sophisticated eye, the rustic animal hospital/supply shop looked like something from the set of an old-fashioned Wild West film, with its wood plank floors, bare wood shelving, and log-cabin walls. But this was no movie set. Creature Comforts was the real deal. You could tell by the smell of animals and feed that filled the room. (Not to mention the lack of cameras and the yummy snacks of a craft services table!) And Darcy, in her designer pink blouse, gray and pink miniskirt, and huge, heart-shaped rhinestone earrings seemed more than slightly out of place.

She *felt* out of place, as well. No matter how hard she tried to get the hang of this laid-back country living thing, Darcy's heart was still firmly planted in Malibu.

"It's definitely going to be the party of the year," Darcy pronounced as she shared the details of Sienna's soiree with her pals Kathi and Lindsay.

Lindsay's dad, Dr. Kevin Adams, owned the Creature Comforts animal clinic. Lindsay and Darcy worked there together. Kathi just liked to hang out.

Darcy wasn't quite sure why Kathi liked to spend her time around horse feed and kitty litter, but she was glad she did. Kathi loved talking about things like parties, clothes, and boys. Lindsay didn't go for that kind of stuff much. She was the serious, hardworking type. Not that there was anything wrong with that or anything. It was just that Darcy wished she would lighten up a little bit. In fact, she'd sort of made that her pet project. She giggled slightly at that. *Pet* project at Creature Comforts. Yeah, that was a good one.

"Last year, Roley Nakamura took us to Catalina Island on hot-air balloons, and we had a treasure hunt for real pearls. See?" Darcy continued as she pulled up her sleeve and revealed a delicate pearl bracelet.

"Wow!" Kathi exclaimed.

"Y'know, pearls are formed when a piece of gunk gets stuck inside an oyster's gut, and it wraps stuff like scar tissue all over it until it becomes a pearl," Lindsay remarked without even glancing up from her work.

"And then it becomes an awesome bracelet," Kathi declared. "And it gets worn by the most glamorous people in the most beautiful places in the world."

"It's still a kidney stone from a mollusk," Lindsay insisted.

Darcy laughed. "And you wouldn't want to go to a party where they gave away mollusk kidney stones?" she teased.

"Okay, I'm sure it would be a blast," Lindsay admitted, tossing her long brown ponytail. "I'm just saying you can have a good party without pearls and hot-air balloons." She looked down at the paperwork lying on the counter in front of her and got back to work. With Lindsay, parties—even the kind with kidney-stone bracelet hunts—came in a very distant second.

Ironically, Darcy's tales of exciting parties weren't having the usual effect on Kathi, either. Ordinarily Kathi hung on Darcy's every word, just dying to hear all the details. But today, Darcy's endless chatter about how wonderful Sienna's big bash was going to be only served to make Kathi feel kind of depressed. In fact, she seemed more interested in Lindsay's uninterested response to Darcy's stories than anything else. She seemed glad to hear that Lindsay felt that bigger parties weren't necessarily better parties. And she had good reason to feel that way.

"Good," Kathi said, " 'cause my birthday's coming up and the only balloons I'm having are the normal, boring kind. But we are having hula punch." She

frowned, knowing how dull that must have sounded
to Darcy.

Before Kathi could spill any more of her party
details, the door opened. Mack McCabe, a local
rancher known mostly for his cantankerous behavior,
strutted into the store. "I've got an order to place," he
barked out as he brandished an order form in the air.
"Is Dr. Adams around?"

"Actually, he got a call a while ago and—" Darcy
began to explain.

But Mack McCabe wanted answers, not explana-
tions. "Is he here or not?" he demanded in a loud,
impatient voice that echoed through the clinic.

Darcy jumped back. *Yikes. This guy is scary.*

But Lindsay didn't seem the least bit intimidated by
the gruff rancher. "He's out delivering a foal, Mr.
McCabe," she told him calmly. "We can take care of
the order."

Darcy looked at the girl with awe. That was
Lindsay. Always in control. *Très* impressive.

"This is important," Mack McCabe insisted. "I
prefer to deal with an adult."

Darcy smiled brightly. "If it helps, Dr. Adams has
frequently said that he has complete confidence in
me," she assured him. She stood tall behind the

counter and gave the rancher her most professional smile.

Mack McCabe stared at Darcy's shimmering pink lip gloss, professionally highlighted hair, and huge rhinestone earrings, and shook his head. Confidence? Instead, he turned toward Lindsay. "I guess *you'll* have to do," he said as he handed her the order form.

As Lindsay glanced down at the piece of paper, Darcy read over her shoulder. While Lindsay seemed nonplussed by the ranch owner's request, Mack McCabe's order form seemed as fascinating as a movie magazine to her. "Two hundred chicks!" Darcy exclaimed knowingly. "Wow! You must be making a music video."

Mack McCabe rolled his eyes. "They're baby chicks, for my ranch," he explained to her.

Darcy blushed prettily but said nothing. What could she say? It had been an honest mistake. After all, the word *chick* could mean a lot of things. It certainly had a different meaning where she came from.

Mack McCabe turned to Lindsay. "She won't be involved in this in any way, right?" he demanded.

"You'll have the chicks by Saturday," Lindsay assured the rancher as she put the finishing touches on his order form.

"I'm out of the county till Monday," he informed her. "Store 'em here at the clinic. Make sure you keep 'em warm!"

As he turned to leave, Darcy smiled at him. "*Hasta la* bye-bye," she said with a friendly grin. "That means *ciao* in Spanish."

Mack McCabe had no answer for that. He just shook his head and walked out the door.

"He seems nice," Darcy commented sincerely.

"He's a grump," Lindsay corrected her. "But he's an important customer, so we have to keep him a happy grump." And to that end, Lindsay hurried to the back room so she could call to order the baby chicks in private.

Once Lindsay was out of the room, Darcy turned her attention toward Kathi. "Well, we're not inviting that happy grump to your party," she informed her authoritatively.

"What do you mean?" Kathi asked.

Darcy smiled at her. "I mean, I'm sure *your* hula punch party would be both fun and unforgettable, but *I'm* throwing your birthday party."

"Really?!" Kathi asked excitedly.

Darcy nodded. "I may not know a lot about oyster guts, but I know a little something about how to host a killer soiree."

Kathi didn't need any convincing. The idea of her new sophisticated California friend planning her party was obviously overwhelming. "This is great!" she squealed, her red hair flying in her face as she jumped wildly around the room. "This is great! This is great!"

Chapter 3

Wild Wisdom . . . *Trout eat a wide variety of things, from aquatic insects and crayfish to small rodents.*

Once Darcy promised to plan Kathi's big birthday bash, she had to get to work. There wasn't much time, and there was plenty to do if she was going to make this a party that was up to Darcy Fields's standards. After all, she had a reputation to live up to. All right, maybe not live up to, since she'd never planned a party in Bailey, but certainly she had to set a new standard in town. It was like her duty or something.

And there was so much to do—choose a theme, plan a menu, and get the decorations together. Not to mention the costumes, invitations, and music. *Wow*. It made her head spin. There was no way Darcy was going to be able to do this on her own. And since there were no party planners around, she would have to enlist the aid of the most organized teen she knew—Lindsay Adams.

Which is why, the next evening, Darcy and Lindsay found themselves in the middle of Darcy's living room, surrounded by a sea of boxes. Each of the cartons was clearly labeled—"Luau," "Disco," "Halloween" . . .

"Okay, the most important part in planning a party is choosing a theme," Darcy explained to Lindsay. "These boxes contain decorations from some of my most successful parties over the last six months." She reached into a huge box and pulled out a silk flower lei. "This box was for a Hawaiian luau party," she explained as she put the lei around Lindsay's neck. Then she pointed to a carton that contained a huge, mirrored silver ball. "And this box was for a '70s disco party," she added.

Lindsay looked incredulously around the room. "Each box is from a party?" she exclaimed. "When did you find time to sleep?"

"During gym class," Darcy replied, surprised that the überintelligent Lindsay couldn't figure that one out for herself.

Before Lindsay could reply, the doorbell rang. Victoria bounded out of the kitchen, eager to see who had arrived.

"I'll get the door," she told the girls as she held a

large wooden spoon to stir the pungent concoction she was creating in a saucepan. "It's such a breath of fresh air, not having a houseful of servants to do everything for us."

Fresh air? Darcy sniffed as her mother passed by with her sour, slightly fishy smelling recipe. *Not exactly.*

"Yup, that was brutal," Darcy replied sarcastically. Still, she had to smile as she caught a glimpse of her mom as she passed. Victoria had tied her hair into pigtails. She looked exactly like what she was . . . a glamorous British actress dressed as a small-town farm girl. It was as though she was playing yet another part . . . and enjoying it immensely.

Victoria opened the door with her free hand and smiled at her guest. "Oh, Dr. Adams, what a pleasure," she said sincerely as Lindsay's father entered the room.

"Hi, Victoria," the veterinarian replied. "I was up at the Zidell ranch vaccinating their sheep and I thought I'd stop by and see if Lindsay needs a ride home." He peered into her saucepan. "Dinner, eh? What's cooking?" he asked as he stuck a finger into the pan and popped a taste into his mouth.

"It's the recipe you gave me for the baby hawk

gruel," Victoria told him proudly. "Dog food, ground-up trout, and steamed bone meal."

Dr. Adams gagged slightly but managed to keep from completely spitting the gruel from his mouth. "They'll love it," he assured her through pursed lips. It was pretty obvious to Darcy that he felt like throwing up, but she knew he wouldn't dare. How un-macho would that be! And Dr. Adams was definitely trying to impress Victoria. That was clear by the way he was smiling at her and trying desperately to act nonchalant. Darcy could tell her mother was also kind of interested in Dr. Adams. Their behavior made it so obvious, Darcy was sure even Lindsay had picked up on the vibe in the room. In fact, the only two who didn't seem to get it were Victoria Fields and Kevin Adams. Darcy sighed. *Grown-ups.* She would never understand them.

"I hope so," Victoria replied, staring at the gray gruel in the pan. She seemed sincerely concerned that the baby birds enjoy the meal she'd cooked up for them, but she was unsure. "I'm afraid the ground-up trout's a bit pungent," she added.

At the mention of fish that might be less than fresh, Dr. Adams swallowed hard, and then turned to his daughter. "You need a ride, Lindsay?" he asked, trying to get his mind off the gross taste in his mouth.

"Lindsay's helping me with Kathi's party," Darcy announced, looking up from the box of Hawaiian grass skirts and floral leis. "You gonna stop by on Saturday, Dr. Adams?"

Lindsay's dad shook his head. "Wish I could. But I just agreed to fill in for the guest speaker in Denver on cattle disease. It's a great opportunity."

"Oh! How exciting," Victoria told him.

Darcy looked at her mother strangely. *Exciting?* Not quite. Exciting was going to the opening of a new club, or walking down a red carpet at a movie premiere. But speaking about cattle disease? *Ugh.*

Still, Dr. Adams seemed pretty thrilled with the idea. "Yes. Luckily for me, the doctor who was supposed to speak got trampled by one of his patients."

"Oh dear," Victoria murmured.

"But Dad," Lindsay interrupted, "Mr. McCabe's chicks are coming in Saturday. They have to be monitored under heat lamps and everything."

"Oh, that's right," Dr. Adams recalled. His mind began to race, searching for a solution to this new dilemma. "Uh . . . hmm . . ."

"Dad, I can take care of it," Lindsay volunteered.

"What, be in charge for the whole weekend? I
don't know. . . ." her father began.

"I don't know, either," Darcy butted in. She
looked at Lindsay in disbelief. "Run the clinic for the
whole weekend? You'd miss the party." She turned to
Dr. Adams. "She's not thinking clearly."

"I can do it," Lindsay continued, blatantly avoiding
Darcy's comments. "Any serious cases I'll refer to Dr.
Lydecker, but I can handle everything else. You can
trust me."

Dr. Adams studied his daughter's face. Finally he
nodded slowly. "Sure I can," he replied. "Okay,
Linds, you're on."

"Great!" Lindsay exclaimed. She leaped away
from the boxes. "Maybe I'll come with you now.
There's some stuff I want to get ready for this
weekend."

"Great," Dr. Adams said. His arms and shoulders
relaxed, as he was clearly relieved to have had his
problems solved so easily.

Well, almost all of his problems, anyway. There
was one issue that even Lindsay, a *très* responsible kid,
couldn't help her father with. It called for far more
powerful assistance. "Before we go, Dad, have a mint.
You've got some trout breath."

Dr. Adams grimaced. He knew what she meant. It would be a while before he could get the taste of that hawk gruel out of his system.

After a few days of party planning, Darcy finally had the theme picked, the decorations made, and the menu set for Kathi's big b-day celebration. With the details pretty set, she felt she was finally ready to send out a press release of her own. Sure, this party wasn't going to make it to the pages of supermarket tabloids or anything, but she did want her friends in California to know that she hadn't completely abandoned the soiree scene. So the next day, while she was at work, Darcy pulled out her laptop and spread the word.

❋ (**DARCY'S DISH**) ❋

Hey, people. Great news. I've settled on a theme for my friend Kathi's party: "Pirates of the Caribbean." Ta-da! But instead of yo-ho-ho and a bottle of rum, it's going to be yo-ho-ho and French manicures. It's going to be great, and everyone's going to be there.

Darcy glanced over the counter and caught a glimpse of Lindsay, who was carefully checking to make sure everything was in order at the clinic before her father left for his conference. Quickly, she typed a correction to her blog.

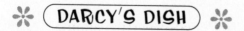

❊ (**DARCY'S DISH**) ❊

Everyone except my friend Lindsay, that is. More later.

❊   ❊   ❊   ❊   ❊   ❊

As Darcy hit the send button on her laptop, she shot Lindsay a sympathetic look.

"What . . . is something in my hair?" Lindsay asked once she felt Darcy's eyes on her.

Darcy shook her head. "I just feel kinda bad."

"I told you not to eat at Stubby's Diner," Lindsay reminded her. "They just let that food sit out."

"No," Darcy corrected her. "I mean, here I am planning Kathi's party right in front of you, and you can't come."

"It's okay," Lindsay said. "I mean, it's kind of cool that my dad trusts me to be in charge, so I don't mind missing the party."

Darcy sighed. Obviously Lindsay wasn't getting the significance of what missing this particular event would mean. "But Lindsay," she explained. "This is a

Darcy Fields party. This is the kind of thing that gets written up in the newspaper." She thought for a moment, considering that idea. "If this town had a newspaper," she added ruefully.

Lindsay shrugged.

But Darcy didn't for a minute believe that Lindsay didn't care about missing the party. After all, nobody missed one of Darcy's parties if they could help it. "Oh, look at you," she said with true compassion. "Putting on a brave face."

"I'm not putting on a brave face," Lindsay insisted. "I really don't mind missing it."

Darcy could hardly stand her friend's courageousness. She reached out her arms and gave her a strong hug. "Oh, honey, you'll be okay," she consoled her.

Chapter 4

Wild Wisdom . . . *Parrots are one of only two animals that can see behind themselves without turning their heads (the other is the rabbit).*

By the time Saturday night arrived, Darcy's party was ready to roll. Her patio had been transformed into an entire high-seas environment, complete with pirate flags, skeletons, ship's flags, and treasure chests overflowing with brightly colored beads and plastic jewels. There was plenty of sushi (fresh from the open seas, of course!), and big barrels of blood-red pirate punch. All of Darcy's new friends were there, and she'd made sure that they were all costumed in cool pirate garb. There were tons of plastic swords, bandannas, pirate hats, and eye patches to go around. Darcy even managed to find herself a pink sequined eye patch.

True to her word, Darcy'd planned for everything . . .

Except the fact that she would be having an unexpected guest. Apparently, her mother had agreed to babysit Lindsay's little brother, Jack, for the weekend while Dr. Adams was away. That was not good news for Darcy. Jack may have looked adorable to the untrained eye, but Darcy knew better. Jack was a troublemaker. He was obsessed with Hollywood, and he saw Darcy and her mother as his way into the movie biz. As a result, he always seemed to be taking pictures of them at their most embarrassing moments. Jack was also kind of a pest—always getting in the way of the things Darcy and Lindsay wanted to do.

As far as Darcy was concerned, if it were up to her, Lindsay's little brother would definitely have been on the other side of the red rope for this party. Unfortunately, it hadn't been up to her. Her mom had pulled rank on that one.

Jack was definitely thrilled to be at the party. "Thanks for baby-sitting me, Mrs. Fields," he told Victoria.

"Not at all, Jack," Victoria replied as she perused the decorations. "Your dad was afraid you'd be kind of a handful, hard to keep an eye on. But I . . ."

As Victoria turned around to smile at Jack, a wave of panic came over her. The kid was gone!

"Jack! Jack!" she shouted as her eyes searched the crowd of swashbuckling, sword-fighting, fast-dancing teenage pirates for some sign of the little guy.

"Woo-hoo!" came his loud, excited answer.

Victoria whirled around quickly, and drew a big sigh of relief as she spotted Jack at the other end of the patio. He was dancing, like some of the older kids were. Only Jack's dancing partner wasn't a teenage girl. He was getting down on the dance floor with a plastic pirate skeleton.

Suddenly, Jack pulled a small digital camera from his pocket and began snapping photos. "A movie star and her daughter at a wild party," he mused. "*Hot Celebrity* magazine will pay top dollar for these babies."

Victoria quickly slipped out of sight behind some flowers. It was an immediate, instinctive reaction. She had a lot of experience with ducking the paparazzi.

As Jack snapped away with his camera, Eli went straight for the food. He came away from the buffet with a plate of hot chicken satay. He held up one of the wooden skewers and smiled at a girl standing nearby. "Here's the key with satay—you have to be careful with the little spears they're on," he told her, trying to sound like a big expert in order to impress her. He demonstrated by gingerly placing a skewer in his mouth.

At just that moment, Jack spotted Eli. He'd known him for years. He slapped him on the back in greeting. "How's it goin'?" Jack asked.

Eli didn't answer. Actually, he *couldn't* answer. That slap on the back had caught him off guard and sent the skewer right down his throat. "Ack!" he gagged, clutching at his neck.

Click! Now *that* was a photo Jack couldn't resist.

At the moment, Darcy was completely unaware that one of her guests had just been stabbed in the throat by a chicken satay skewer. She had other troubles on her mind.

"Thank you for having this party, Darcy," Kathi said as the girls sipped some pirate punch. "Shiver me timbers," she added, in her best pirate voice.

"You bet," Darcy replied. Then she added, "*arrr,*" for good measure. But she didn't sound convincing. It was obvious her mind was elsewhere.

"Are you okay?" Kathi asked.

"I just feel bad about Lindsay. I mean, here we are having this great party, and she's stuck at Creature Comforts."

"I know. It's like she's Cinderella, missing the . . ."

Kathi thought for a moment. "Pirate ball," she said finally. "And her hook doesn't fit the other guy's glove, so at midnight the pirate ship turns into a . . . parrot."

Darcy looked at Kathi strangely. Then she nodded. "That's exactly right," she agreed. "I mean, the Cinderella part. All of the pirate stuff, I don't know what that was."

Kathi blushed slightly.

"Lindsay is like Cinderella," Darcy continued. "And do you know what that makes me?"

"Captain Hook!" Kathi answered proudly.

"No," Darcy told her patiently. "You're back on the pirate thing." A familiar smile flashed across her lips. Her face looked the way it always did when a plan was forming in her mind. "It makes me Lindsay's fairy godmother."

While Darcy hatched her new plan at the party, back at Creature Comforts, Cinderella . . . uh . . . er . . . Lindsay, was taking care of some recently hatched chicks. She'd placed all two hundred of the fuzzy baby birds in a safe wire pen and was getting ready to turn in for a peaceful evening.

"There you go, chickies," Lindsay said as she adjusted the heat lamp over the pen. "All warm and cozy. Let's have a nice quiet night."

But Darcy had other ideas. At just that moment, the doors to the clinic burst open, and a swarm of kids in pirate costumes streamed in with a boom box, treasure chests, plastic skeletons, and containers of blood-red pirate punch in hand.

"Hoist anchor and let the party set sail!" Darcy announced in her best pirate accent.

Kathi plugged the boom box into a nearby outlet and music began to blare throughout the clinic. Within seconds the party was back on. The kids began to eat, dance, and have sword fights. It was as if no one even noticed the change in venue.

Except Lindsay, of course. "Darcy, you can't have a party here!" she shouted out over the blaring tunes.

"You couldn't come to the party, so the party's coming to you!" Darcy explained happily.

"But this is a veterinary clinic," Lindsay insisted. She pointed across the room. The kids were going wild. "Look at Terry Nolan. He's messing up the flea collars. Sarah Follet's playing with a pitchfork, and Eli's . . ." she stopped for a minute and stared as Eli moved around the room, wildly jerking his arms up and down while kicking his legs in the opposite direction. "What exactly is Eli doing?" she asked Darcy.

"He's dancing, I think," she replied, watching for a moment as Eli flailed his limbs some more. Actually, she wasn't quite sure if dancing was the word for it. Still . . . "Well, he's doing *something*," she added. "The point is, he's having fun. We all are."

"I'm not," Lindsay corrected her.

"Well, you haven't had any snacks yet," Darcy told her. She handed Lindsay a large wooden tray filled with rows and rows of brightly colored sushi rolls. "And I know you prefer country music, but I'm sure I brought along a CD with some of that boot-scooting, line-dancing stuff."

Lindsay shook her head. "You don't get it, Malibu. My dad left me in charge. These people have to get out." She sounded very serious. *Seriously angry*.

Darcy looked at her friend strangely. A normal person would be thrilled to have one of Darcy's parties delivered straight to her doorstep. And this party was totally rocking. Which gave rise to the question: Didn't Lindsay ever like to have a good time?

"What's the big deal?" Darcy asked her pointedly. "It's just some kids having fun for Kathi's birthday."

Lindsay sighed. "Okay, true, but . . ." she began.

"And this is the only way you can be at the party," Darcy continued. "I bet your dad wouldn't want you to miss it."

"Well . . . maybe," Lindsay replied slowly.

"*Definitely*," Darcy corrected her. "Besides, it's not like anything bad is going to happen."

Darcy and her friends were having a great time pirate partying at the clinic, but that didn't mean much to Jack. Unfortunately for him, Victoria had insisted her charge stay at the ranch, where she could keep an eye on him. Jack had been left behind. And he wasn't at all happy about it.

"Movie star, movie star's daughter," he muttered sadly to himself as he studied some of the pictures he'd taken earlier. Darcy's backside, the top of Victoria's head peeking over some shrubbery . . . "Movie star's daughter's party." He sighed sadly. "Happier times . . ."

But Jack shouldn't have been so depressed. Actually, the mop-topped boy *hadn't* been forgotten at all. In fact, Victoria had *special* plans for him.

"All right, Jack my boy!" she called out enthusiastically as she entered the living room carrying a huge wooden box. "Ready to have some fun?"

Jack perked up immediately. "Are we going to Creature Comforts with everyone else?" he asked excitedly.

Victoria shook her head and placed the box down. "No. We're going to feed baby birds."

A flicker of hope flashed across Jack's face. "Really?! Who are we gonna feed 'em to?"

"We're going to feed them with an eyedropper," Victoria explained.

"Oh," Jack sighed. Any glimmer of excitement disappeared instantly from his face. He glanced back at the photos he had taken. "Movie star's hired hand choking on meat skewer." He laughed as he studied the photo of Eli gagging on his chicken satay. "Heh-heh-heh. That was good."

"Buck up, Jack," Victoria urged. "This is the wonder of nature." She looked down into the box. There were the three tiny baby hawks that had just hatched in her incubator.

Jack shook his head slightly. "Mrs. Fields, I grew up in the wonder of nature. I live over a veterinary clinic." He raised his hand to his chin. "I'm up to here with the wonder of nature. I want to be up to here in a hot tub in Hollywood."

"You have delicate skin, Jack. You'd get all

pruney," Victoria joked. "Now, hold the eyedropper while I get the puppet." She handed him a small eyedropper filled with baby hawk gruel, then walked over to the counter to pick up a felt hand puppet.

"There's a puppet?" Jack asked with surprise.

Victoria sat down beside him and placed the puppet on her hand. It was gray and white like a hawk, with two felt wings on its sides. "We have to feed the babies with a puppet of their mother so the babies won't imprint humans as their parents," she explained. "That way, when we return them to the wild, they can function with other hawks."

But Jack had a better idea. "Why *not* have them think we're their parents?" he asked in a slightly devious voice. "Then they'd be our servants and we could have them attack our enemies." He raised his hands up and let them float in front of him, as though he were laying out a movie marquee. "I'd be Jack, Warlord of the Hawk People."

Victoria wasn't going for it. Somehow, the idea of Jack as a warlord over any creature seemed like a dangerous idea. "I'll wear the puppet," she told him. "You can stir the fish gruel."

Chapter 5

While Jack and Victoria fed the baby hawks, the kids at Creature Comforts were having a feeding frenzy of their own. And their menu was a lot more delicious than any trout and bone meal gruel. At the moment, they were chowing down on sushi, satay, and, of course, birthday cake. Even Lindsay seemed to be snacking on some of the food. It actually seemed that Darcy had been right. Everyone was having a blast. It wasn't like anything bad was happening. . . .

Famous last words.

Suddenly, something *very, very* bad happened. One of the dancing teens somehow managed to trip over the chick pen. The metal cage tipped over and its door swung open. Within seconds, two hundred yellow cheeping chicks flooded through the party.

Lindsay gasped as soon as she spotted the chicks. They were everywhere. And they were fast! This was exactly what she'd been afraid of. "I can't believe this!" Lindsay shouted out furiously. "Mr. McCabe is going to freak. My dad's gonna kill me!" She stormed away angrily, heading across the room to stand the cage upright again.

Darcy wasn't too happy about it, either. What a mess! *Two hundred chicks loose.* And not marshmallow Peeps, either. These were the real deal. She had not planned on chicks wandering around her dance floor— at least, not the little yellow kind with feathers, wings, and beaks. This was a total emergency! Darcy closed her eyes and tried to breathe. "Whoa. Whoa. Deep breath," she murmured as she tried to regain her composure.

That deep breathing must have worked miracles because suddenly, an idea came to her. "We'll catch the chicks," she blurted out. "It'll be fun!" Darcy seemed very pleased with herself. It was the perfect plan. After all, if Roley Nakamura could have her party guests look for oyster kidney stones, Darcy Fields could have hers catch live chicks. "Okay, everybody!" she announced to everyone in the room. "Pirate Treasure Hunt. Whoever picks up the most chicks wins."

"That's what my Uncle Breezy says," Kathi remarked with a knowing nod.

"Okay, everybody, go!" Darcy shouted out.

The contest was on! Kids scattered all around the clinic, chasing the chicks under tables, behind doors, and onto shelves. There was no place they wouldn't look.

Eli sprawled under a table full of cat food cans. He reached out his arm and managed to grab one of the wayward chicks. He leaped up, triumphantly . . . and flipped over the table. Cans of cat food rolled all over the floor.

Kathi grabbed a long-handled butterfly net to trap the little yellow birds as they ran. Unfortunately, all she managed to trap in her net was Eli. He moved his arms furiously as he tried to free himself from the netting. Surprisingly, it didn't look all that different from his dancing technique.

A few chicks waddled over to a nearby feed bin. A group of kids dove at them at once, each trying to catch as many of the little yellow birds as they could. The kids missed the chicks, but they did hit the spout of the bin, sending feed to stream out all over the floor.

One party guest chased a chick to the corner of the room. She bumped into a shelf and knocked over a bottle of horse shampoo. The shampoo poured out all over Darcy, covering her new shirt.

But it was *Lindsay* who got angry. "Okay, cut it out!" she demanded. "STOP IT!"

Darcy couldn't believe it. Why was Lindsay trying to stop things just when the party was getting exciting? Everyone was loving the chick hunt. Now Lindsay was ruining everything. "What's the problem?" Darcy demanded.

"*What's the problem?*" Lindsay repeated in disbelief. "My dad left me in charge, and the place is getting trashed!"

"Lindsay, it's no biggie," Darcy assured her. She was beginning to get annoyed with Lindsay's total party-pooper attitude.

"No biggie?!" Lindsay yelled back. "You wouldn't know a biggie if it bit you in the behind!"

"Relax. Everybody's having fun," Darcy countered.

That just made Lindsay more angry. "Fun?!" she demanded. "That's all you think about."

"At least I think about fun!" Darcy countered. "All you do is work."

"I work because I'm responsible," Lindsay
explained. She threw her hands up in the air. "Just
forget it!" she shouted as she stormed off in search of
a broom to clean up the mess.

A week ago, it would have been impossible to
predict the way that Darcy's party would turn out.
And it would have been shocking to imagine that the
real fun was actually going on back at Darcy's house.
But this was the way things had turned out. While
Darcy was miserably fighting with Lindsay, Victoria
and Jack were having a blast feeding the baby hawks.

"There you go," Victoria cooed as she fed the
baby hawks gruel through an eyedropper. "That's
some yummy ground trout and bone meal." Two of
the birds came up to the mother hawk hand puppet
without any fear at all. But the third one didn't seem
to have the same reaction to the puppet. "Hmmm . . .
this little one's not eating," she remarked with concern.

"Talk to it the way you did to the little kids in
one of my favorite movies, *Orphans of Rangoon*,"
Jack suggested, referring to one of Victoria's films.

"Jack, I was on allergy medicine for that entire
movie," Victoria admitted. "I can't remember a word

I said."

Luckily Jack could recall every word of dialogue perfectly. "You told the kids, 'Do it. Not for me, but for your parents and your ancestors and the spirit of your country,' " he repeated, in his best imitation of a British accent.

Victoria considered Jack's idea for a moment. Then she decided to give it a try. She held the mommy hawk hand puppet and the eyedropper right above the little hawk's head. "Do it. Not for me . . . et cetera. But for the spirit of your country."

Jack peered nervously into the box, waiting to see if Victoria's abbreviated version of the speech had been enough to persuade the little bird to drink some of the gooey gruel from the dropper. Sure enough, the baby hawk tilted his head, opened his beak, and began swallowing the mixture.

"It's working! He's eating!" Jack shouted excitedly. He grabbed a nearby sock and put it on his hand like a puppet. "Here, I wanna help!" he told Victoria. He began waving his sock puppet over the heads of the baby hawks. "I'm a worm," he said in a small, puppet-like voice. "One day you'll grow big and eat me."

Victoria giggled. "Very good, Jack."

Jack stood up and spread his arms wide. "And then

you'll owe your allegiance to Jack, Warlord of the Hawk People!" he exclaimed in his most powerful voice.

Victoria placed her hawk puppet beside the worm and began acting out a scene of her own, making the hawk puppet chow down on its delicious worm puppet dinner. It was dinner theater for hawks, and those lucky just-hatched babies had a front-row-seat.

Much to his own surprise, Jack was actually having a very good time acting out scenes with Victoria. It was just like being on a Hollywood movie set—except for the fact that there were no cameras anywhere and the house smelled like rotten trout. But to him, this was a dream come true. His creative mind was bursting with ideas for adventure and intrigue—all of which he was acting out with sock puppets. Best of all, he was hanging out with a genuine Hollywood star. Even fermented fish couldn't dull his excitement.

Chapter 6

Wild Wisdom . . . *Scorpions have six to twelve eyes—but terrible eyesight.*

There was plenty of excitement going on at Creature Comforts, too. But no one would be able to say that Jack's older sister was having any fun. There were baby chicks everywhere, and the mess in the clinic seemed to have taken on a life of its own. There was a sticky mixture of animal feed mixed with horse shampoo all over the floor. Dog leashes and cans of cat food had been knocked off their shelves. And worst of all, the little chicks were making a huge mess. After all, chickens can't be house-trained. Lindsay would be cleaning up their droppings for days to come, she just knew it.

Finally, Lindsay became absolutely fed up with the way Darcy had hijacked her weekend with her pirate party. "Okay, everybody, just go home!" she demanded. "I'll catch the rest of the chicks and get this mess cleaned up before my dad gets home."

Too late.

At just that moment, Dr. Adams opened the door of the clinic. From the look on his face, it was obvious that he was not pleased with what was going on inside.

"I caught an early flight back," Dr. Adams said, stepping aside to avoid being trampled by partygoers eager to leave and avoid a scene between Lindsay and her dad. "I figured you'd still be able to get to Kathi's party for a couple of hours." He glanced around the room, getting angrier and angrier with each passing second. "I see I didn't have to worry about *that*," he said, not bothering to mask his growing anger.

A moment later, Dr. Adams noticed Eli trying to slog his way out the door. Unfortunately, his movement was severely hampered by the big box currently attached to his foot.

"What's on Eli's foot?" Dr. Adams asked.

"It's a humane raccoon trap, sir," Eli explained. "I'm stuck in it. I'll bring it back tomorrow."

Dr. Adams sighed heavily as Eli limped out of the clinic.

"Dad, I can explain," Lindsay began.

"I'm not sure there is an explanation for Eli," Dr. Adams replied as he watched the door close.

"I meant this mess," Lindsay explained.

Dr. Adams shook his head. "You know, I don't care how the mess got started," he told Lindsay. "All I know is you asked me to trust you, I trusted you, and you had a party at our clinic."

"But . . ." Lindsay began.

Her father refused to let her finish. "I don't want to hear it," he interrupted her. "You trashed the place, you let a pen full of chicks loose, you jeopardized our relationship with a very important customer, and you proved that you're not responsible." The exasperated vet reached into his pocket and pulled out a bizarre-looking lump of glass with a nasty-looking insect-type creature trapped inside. "And now I don't feel like giving you the scorpion paperweight I brought you from Denver."

Lindsay looked from her dad's disappointed face to the scorpion paperweight and back again. There was nothing she could say. There was nothing *anyone* could say that would excuse this.

Of course, having nothing to say had never stopped Darcy before. She had to help Lindsay . . . even if it meant getting herself in trouble.

"It's not her fault. It's my fault," Darcy blurted out suddenly.

"What?" Dr. Adams asked, surprised.

"What?" Lindsay echoed.

"I brought the party here," Darcy continued. "Lindsay tried to make us go home, but I said it would be fine. And when the chicks got loose, I said it would be fun, and everything got all messed up."

Dr. Adams turned and studied Lindsay's face. She seemed almost as surprised at Darcy's outburst as he was.

"Don't be mad at her," Darcy continued. "She kept trying to stop it, but I wouldn't let her. So you don't have to give me my scorpion paperweight." She stopped for a minute, realizing that she'd just asked for a gift . . . not a good thing. *Especially in a situation like this.* "I mean, if you brought me one," she added quietly.

"I didn't," Dr. Adams replied a bit sheepishly. He reached into his coat pocket and pulled out a jar with a bright red label. "I got you chili fixin's." He handed the jar to Darcy, then turned his attention back to Lindsay. "I guess I owe you an apology."

"No, you don't," Lindsay assured him. "You put me in charge, and I let it happen." Her face fell. "I let you down," she added sadly.

But Dr. Adams wasn't angry anymore. Instead, he had a Dadlike grin on his face—the kind parents get when their kids do something really wonderful that surprises them. Seeing that look on Dr. Adams's face *right now* certainly surprised Darcy!

"You're taking responsibility," Dr. Adams explained to his daughter. "Right now. I know you tried to stop it. Next time, I'm sure you will." He reached over and handed her the paperweight. "Here, have a scorpion," he added, sounding as though he were giving Lindsay a trophy. "And don't worry. He died of natural causes."

"Thanks, Dad," Lindsay replied gratefully. She studied the dead eight-legged creature with a fascination Darcy *totally* didn't get. "I'll do better next time."

Dr. Adams had no doubt of that. He reached over and gave her a big hug.

Cheep. Cheep.

Dr. Adams pulled away from Lindsay and looked down. There were chick noises coming from his coat. He reached into his front pocket and, sure enough, produced a tiny ball of yellow fluff. "How'd you get in there?" Dr. Adams asked the little chick.

"Those chicks are sneaky-fast," Darcy told him.

And she should know. After all, there was one climbing around inside her pirate hat right now. She reached up and grabbed him on the first try. She smiled triumphantly. Another chick caught. She was going to win this competition yet!

Chapter 7

Wild Wisdom . . . *Warthogs sometimes mark their territories by rubbing a substance that comes from glands near their eyes against objects.*

Dr. Adams may have been surprised by Darcy's party, but he was no more shocked than Darcy would have been had she any idea what her mother and Jack were up to back at the ranch.

At that very moment, Victoria and Jack were busy putting on a very elaborate puppet production for the entertainment of the hawk babies. Victoria was now wearing two puppets, one on each hand. She had the hawk puppet on her right hand and a princess puppet, complete with yellow yarn hair, button eyes, and red, red lipstick, on her left.

Jack had a created a sock puppet with a cape and a crown, which he had named Jack, Warlord of the Hawk People . . . *naturally.*

"I, Jack, Warlord of the Hawk People, command

you, Mighty Hawk, to rescue Princess Portabello
from the Evil Emperor Warthog." He held up a big,
plush brown warthog hand puppet with a snout and
bulging eyes. When Darcy had gotten him, back when
she was a little girl, she'd thought he was just a cute
fuzzy puppet. Somehow, Jack had managed to turn
him into a princess-stealing, hawk-eating villain—the
Evil Emperor Warthog.

"Mighty Hawk shall obey," Victoria replied in her
most heroic voice as she lifted the hawk puppet and
prepared to battle with Jack's warthog puppet.

"Never!" Jack made the warthog declare with a
villainous laugh. "Princess Portabello is my prisoner,
and I will only release her for a huge sum of riches.
And a jet!"

But the Princess Portabello puppet had other
plans. She grabbed a candle and conked the Evil
Emperor Warthog on the hand.

"Ow!" Jack shouted. Forget the warthog. It was
his hand that stung.

"Now you know the wrath of my candle," Victoria
made Princess Portabello say. She turned her hand
puppets toward each other. "Take me home, Mighty
Hawk." She rested one hand on top of the other so it
looked as if the hawk puppet was flying with the

princess puppet on its back. "You have rescued me, Warlord Jack," she continued as the two puppets soared through the air. "And for that, I will marry you and become Queen." She reached out her hand so Princess Portabello could plant a big, juicy puppet kiss on Warlord Jack.

The real Jack scowled. Romance puppet shows definitely weren't his thing. "Yuck! Enough of that!" he declared. "The End!"

Victoria giggled and put down her puppets. "It's getting late, anyway," she said as she glanced down into the box. "The birds fell asleep half an hour ago."

"Okay," Jack agreed, removing his puppets as well. But his mind was already moving ahead toward his next production. "For tomorrow's show, I'm thinking an earthquake and a shipwreck . . ."

Victoria shook her head. "I'm sorry, Jack. I'm afraid the babies go back into the nest tomorrow."

Jack's face fell. "Oh."

"Don't be disappointed, Jack," Victoria said, trying to cheer him up. "Be proud. Look at these wonderful birds you've helped save."

Jack looked down into the box. The little hawk babies were fast asleep. "Yeah, I guess that's pretty cool. . . ."

"I'd say so," Victoria agreed. She gazed down

lovingly at the tiny creatures. It was clear she was amazed at how miraculous they really were.

But the sight of Victoria and the hawks brought other things to mind for Jack. He pulled out his camera and snapped a picture. "Movie star saves nature," he said, imagining the headline. A greedy smile flashed across his little face. "Ka-ching!"

Back at Creature Comforts, Darcy and Lindsay were finally almost finished cleaning things up. Unfortunately, it also seemed as though their friendship might be finished as well. The two had been cleaning for hours in complete silence.

But Darcy just couldn't let that happen! She liked Lindsay. A lot. She couldn't let one little party get in the way of their friendship. She had to say something.

"My friend Shelby's parents once went two and a half months without talking to each other," she told Lindsay.

Lindsay shot her a look, but kept sweeping piles of animal feed into her dustpan.

"They had some argument about something and the next day they both felt bad about it, but they couldn't figure out how to talk about it. And you

know how the longer you don't talk, the harder it is to
ever talk. It just went on and on," Darcy continued.

Lindsay shrugged. "Uh-huh," she said quietly.

"Anyway," Darcy continued. "That's why I want
to be the first to say I'm sorry." She stood there for a
moment, waiting for Lindsay's reaction.

"I'm sorry, too," Lindsay finally replied. "You're
not thoughtless and you're not self-absorbed and . . ."

"Oh, but I am," Darcy insisted. "I'm all those
things. I'm just really lucky to know you. I might
learn just enough responsibility to keep out of juvey."

The girls both had to smile at that one. The idea
of a fashion plate like Darcy in a plain prison uniform
was too much for either of them to imagine. "Well,
I'll teach you responsibility if you'll teach me how to
lighten up a little," Lindsay said slowly.

"Deal," Darcy agreed.

"Y'know," Lindsay began, a slight flicker of
amusement suddenly coming into her eyes, "the
Darcy in me says we should take a little break and go
grab some ice cream."

Darcy stopped sweeping for a moment to consider
the idea. "The Lindsay in me has to think about
that," she said slowly. Then, after a beat she added,
"The Lindsay in me says, 'Shyeah!' "

Chapter 8

Wild Wisdom . . . *Some hawks can attain speeds of 150 mph while diving.*

The next morning, Darcy, Lindsay, and Kathi were gathered at the Fields' house for another big celebration. But this one didn't include any balloons, pirate hats, or sushi snacks. It wasn't a birthday party, after all. It was more of a celebration of nature. The baby hawks were ready to go back to their nest and meet their mom.

Victoria had been sorry to see the baby hawks leave her home, but she felt really wonderful when she placed them in their nest and prepared them to meet their real mother. "There we go, my little friends," she said as she stood on a ladder and gently placed pieces of real broken hawk eggs in the nest around the baby hawks. "Your momma will see the broken eggshells and think that she hatched you, and she'll start feeding you." She glanced down toward Jack and winked. "You won't be getting the entertaining dinner theater along with it," she continued to tell the hawk babies, "but I think this is best. And for my part, no more pesticides on this ranch!" she vowed as she headed slowly back down the ladder.

Kathi turned to Darcy. "I wanted to say thank you for my party," she remarked gratefully. "It was . . . different. But it was the best party I've ever been to."

"Yeah, me too," Lindsay agreed.

Darcy grinned broadly. "Yeah, me three." She paused for a minute, reconsidering that one. "I'm sorry," she told her friends. "That's crazy. I've been to way better parties. But this was definitely the best party I've been to in *this* town."

"And Jacky's got the pictures to prove it!" Jack piped up, as he strode triumphantly over to the girls with a big grin on his face. He held up his camera.

"Really?" Lindsay asked. She took the camera and began clicking through the pics.

"There's a great one of Darcy stuffing her face," Jack told her. "*Hot Celebrity* magazine is gonna pay me a ton!"

"You took pictures of Mom and me?" Darcy demanded angrily. "And you're going to sell them?"

Jack nodded proudly. It was all part of his grand scheme to become a famous Hollywood mogul. Someday he wanted to be a director, but for now, selling pictures of Darcy and Victoria would have to do.

Unfortunately for him, his sister had a different plan.

"Delete. Delete. Delete," Lindsay said as she got rid of each picture. She smiled at Darcy. "No, he's not."

"Hey," Jack demanded, reaching for his camera.

"You want to take a picture of something worth-while, Jack?" Victoria asked. She pointed to the top of the tree. The mother hawk was soaring above, heading straight for her nest.

Darcy looked up. The hawk really was magnifi-cent, with its gray and white wings fully spread as it soared gracefully through the air below the bright blue cloudless sky. It *would* make a wonderful photo.

But not as far as Jack was concerned. "I can't make any money off that," Jack told Darcy with total disdain.

"Fine," Darcy said, grabbing the camera from Lindsay. "I'll take the picture." Darcy snapped away, preserving the moment when the mother hawk took her first look at her babies.

Forget about circus parties on the beach. This was something to celebrate!

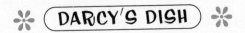

Yo-ho-ho . . . whoa!

Ahoy, maties! I am proud to report that my pirate party was the total talk of the town! It's been a week since the chick-chasing festivities (never mind, you sort of had to be there!) and I still can't walk down the hall at school without someone thanking me for letting them in on all the action! I guess it was the first time anyone in Bailey ever scarfed down blood-red pirate punch before. I am proud to report that, as usual, I have set a new standard for parties . . . at least in this town!

TTYL

Chapter 9

Wild Wisdom . . . *A single brown bat can catch twelve hundred mosquito-sized insects in just one hour.*

Unfortunately, not everybody had gotten the chance to sample Darcy's style of Hollywood hospitality. She'd invited just about every kid she'd met since she'd arrived in Bailey. But being new in town, there were still one or two kids Darcy hadn't yet met. And those poor souls hadn't had a chance to attend a genuine Darcy Fields party.

Take Layne Haznoy, for instance. When he wandered into Creature Comforts about a week after the soirée of the century, Darcy had no idea who he was. She was pretty certain she'd never seen this tall, skinny teenager with an awful taste in clothing before. There was no way she would have forgotten him. After all, he had to be wearing the ugliest orange and yellow Hawaiian shirt Darcy had ever seen. And his pet carrier was so plain. Just blue plastic with wire mesh in the front. Nothing like the Louis Vuitton pet carriers people like Jessica Simpson and Paris Hilton (not to mention a few of Darcy's Malibu buds) were sporting these days.

Still, even fashion-backward customers deserved the very best service. "Welcome to Creature Comforts. I'm Darcy," she introduced herself to him.

Layne was well aware of who Darcy was. After all, it wasn't often that a movie star's daughter moved to Bailey. In fact, this was the only time it had ever happened. And Layne, being the movie buff that he was, had definitely taken notice.

"I know," Layne assured her. "I heard you and your mom moved into Old Man Mercer's ranch. Is your room upstairs or downstairs?"

"Upstairs."

"That's where he died," Layne told her excitedly. He was certain she'd be impressed with his knowledge about her house.

Darcy was not impressed. In fact, she was kind of grossed out. Who wants to sleep where some old guy died? Quickly, she turned and started toward the back room of the clinic. "Lindsay!" she called out in a voice that was clearly begging for help.

"So you're from Hollywood," Layne continued, obviously unaware of Darcy's discomfort. Suddenly, he began to tilt his head in an unnatural position and roll his eyes around in his head. "Very *shagadelic*, baby!" he commented. Then he smiled proudly. "That's my Austin Powers," he exclaimed.

Darcy sighed. This kid had quite possibly the worst fake British accent she'd ever heard. She could only imagine what a real Englishwoman, like her mother, would have thought of it.

Naturally, Darcy was very relieved when Lindsay finally appeared in the room. Now she could pass the kid off on to her. "This gentleman here needs attention," she told Lindsay quickly.

Layne leaned over the counter and tilted his head in his best imitation of a man of mystery. "My name's Haznoy. Layne Haznoy," he said, doing an imitation of James Bond that was even worse than his Austin Powers impersonation.

"I know, Layne," Lindsay replied with an unimpressed sigh. "You're in my history class."

"Layne seems to be having a little trouble with his pet," Darcy interrupted, hoping to speed things along. The sooner Lindsay could check over the animal, the sooner this kid could go on his shagadelic, 007 way.

"Alicia has a little rash on her belly," Layne explained.

Lindsay put on a pair of thick protective yellow gloves, opened the pet carrier, and gently reached inside. Slowly, she pulled out a dark creature with big brownish-black wings and a small, rat-like face.

Darcy gasped and closed her eyes. She opened her mouth to scream in terror, but nothing came out except a high-pitched squeak.

"She's a bat," Layne said proudly.

"She's a BAT!" Darcy screamed out in fear as she finally got her voice back.

"I named her Alicia," Layne explained, seemingly oblivious to the fact that Darcy was petrified and that Lindsay was struggling to keep the bat under control, " 'cause Alicia Silverstone played Batgirl. I thought she was smokin'." Layne's imitation of Jim Carrey in *The Mask* was no better than his Austin Powers or his James Bond, but he didn't seem to care.

"Darcy, can you hold Alicia's wings?" Lindsay asked.

Darcy looked at her strangely. *Duh?* "No." She shook her head wildly. Lindsay nodded just as forcefully. Darcy shook her head even harder. Lindsay nodded once again. This was getting ridiculous. It was also giving Darcy quite a headache.

"It's okay," Layne assured Darcy. "She might look a little weird, but bats are very helpful. They eat bugs."

"So does my cousin Stevie, but I don't like hanging out with him," Darcy said as she stared at the creepy-looking creature while its giant wings fluttered forcefully up and down. She'd seen bats in the movies before, and they'd looked kind of creepy. But that was nothing compared to how they looked in real life. She definitely did not want to touch this thing.

But as Darcy got a glimpse of the stern expression on Lindsay's face, she knew there was no getting out of this. "Okay, okay," she relented as she slipped on a pair of protective gloves and held down the bat's wings while Lindsay examined its belly.

"Well, I don't see anything wrong," Lindsay said after a thorough examination.

"Really?" Layne replied. "It must have cleared up, like that boil I had on my lip."

Darcy winced. That image was almost as gross as holding a bat's wings. "So can I let go of Alicia now?" she asked hopefully.

Lindsay nodded and took Alicia from her. Darcy watched as Lindsay expertly placed the bat back in her pet carrier and locked the door. Lindsay was very impressive. She didn't seem the least bit grossed out by handling the bat.

"What do I owe you?" Layne asked Lindsay.

"There's nothing wrong with her. You don't owe us anything," Lindsay replied.

Layne placed his pinky against his mouth and curled up his lip slightly. " 'Cause I could pay up to *one million dollars*." He smiled at the girls. "That's my Dr. Evil."

"Uh-huh," Lindsay said, obviously indifferent about this latest impersonation. "You can take Alicia home."

But Layne wasn't quite ready to go home. He seemed determined to try his Dr. Evil impression one more time. He touched his pinky to his lip, rolled his eyes and said, " 'Cause I—"

"Go," Lindsay told him, more forcefully.

Even Dr. Evil would have been too afraid to stay after getting a good look at the expression on Lindsay's face. Layne picked up his pet carrier and dashed out of the clinic.

Darcy waited for a moment before nervously asking Lindsay, "Is the bat gone?"

Lindsay nodded.

"So can I freak out now?" Darcy continued.

"Go for it."

Darcy's whole body began to shake. She'd been holding in this massive freak-out for far too long. She stamped her feet. She shook her head. And she let out a wild, bloodcurdling, totally grossed-out scream, "Ugggggghhhhh—eeeeeeohhhhh—ooooghh—gluhhhhh!"

There. That feels so much better.

Victoria's day didn't seem to be going any better than her daughter's. She was having some serious problems in her garden. And even after a day of intensive labor, she seemed no closer to solving it than she had been that morning.

Later that afternoon, as Eli and Darcy watched intently, the former actress reached deep into the rich soil of her garden and yanked out two half-eaten carrots. She held them up and stared at them disdainfully. "So you see, Eli," Victoria told the farmhand. "We have a mole."

Eli expertly examined the half-chewed carrots and declared authoritatively, "You sure do."

Victoria sighed. "And I'm persuaded to believe that's a bad thing."

"It wasn't for Cindy Crawford," Darcy commented. "Her mole made her a fortune."

"Moles aren't that bad. I mean, sure, they burrow into the . . ." Eli began. He stopped for a minute and grinned, suddenly understanding Darcy's little joke. "Oh, I get it. Cindy Crawford has that cute mole on her cheek. That's funny." He chuckled to himself.

Darcy smiled. Eli may have been a little slow on the uptake, but he did recognize a good joke when he heard one.

"I propose we get rid of this mole," Victoria stated, bringing everyone back to the task at hand. She bent down and picked up a long green metal cylinder. "Do you recognize this?"

"Sure," Eli said, taking it from her. "It's a sonic mole repeller. You stick it in the ground and it makes a noise they don't like. Here . . ." He expertly flipped the switch on the side of the repeller to On. He waited a moment, but nothing happened. "It doesn't seem to be working," Eli continued as he examined the device by shaking it close to his ear.

HAROOOOOOOOOOOOOOOO!

Suddenly the mole repeller let out a hideous screeching howl, right into Eli's ear.

"AAAAGGHHHH!" Eli shouted in agony. He dropped the repeller, grabbed his ears, and staggered away. But as he walked off, his foot got caught in some twine that had been set up to help the green bean plants grow. To keep from tripping, the klutzy farmhand tried to steady himself with his other foot, but he stepped into a wire tomato plant cone and . . . *SPLAT*! He landed facedown in the watering trough.

Darcy couldn't help but laugh at that. "Well, it keeps *Eli* out of our garden," she giggled.

Victoria chuckled. "Perhaps we should bring in an expert," she called over to Eli. "He can trap the mole and release it elsewhere."

An upraised thumb slowly rose out from the watering trough. Obviously, Eli agreed. A professional trapper was *definitely* the best plan of action.

Chapter 10

Wild Wisdom . . . *A group of ferrets is called a "business of ferrets."*

"You wouldn't believe the nightmare I had," Darcy said, shuddering as she described her terrifying dream to Lindsay and Kathi. The girls were together at Creature Comforts after school. Darcy busied herself by unwrapping a large package as she spoke, as if keeping active would erase the horrible nightmare from her consciousness. "I was in Paris for Fashion Week," she continued, "and all the runway models changed into vampire bats, and they flapped their wings in my face and chased me up the Eiffel Tower."

"I dreamed I was putting salve on a cow," Lindsay mentioned.

Darcy looked at her, surprised. "Why would you dream that?"

Lindsay shrugged. "Because I spent all day putting salve on a cow."

"And that was the whole dream?" Darcy asked.

Lindsay thought about that for a moment. Finally, she recalled another detail. "The cow said, 'Thank you.'"

Darcy didn't reply. Instead, she pulled a lavender silk blouse from the box she'd been busy unwrapping. "Well, here's my reward for having Layne Haznoy's bat scare the pants off me," she announced triumphantly as she held the shirt up against her body. It actually looked quite good with the formfitting jeans Darcy was wearing. The blouse would be perfect for school, a date, or even work. Once again, Darcy had made a successful purchase.

"So, if something unpleasant happens to you, you just buy stuff?" Kathi deduced, as she thought through what Darcy had just explained.

"Yeah," Darcy replied.

"That's so cool!" Kathi exclaimed, once again completely in awe of the Darcy Fields method of survival. She did have one question for her, though. "What about when something good happens to you?"

Darcy shrugged. "Ah," she said slowly. "Then I buy stuff."

Of course.

"Dolce and Gabbana have been my best friends in times of crises," Darcy continued as she walked into the back room of the clinic and shut the door. "And I'm sure in years to come, there will be no pitfalls in my life's path that our country's great fashion designers won't be able to smooth over with truly wonderful products."

No sooner had she finished her statement than she reemerged from the back room wearing her new acquisition. Kathi and Lindsay marveled at the speed with which Darcy could change her clothes. It was a remarkable skill.

"This blouse, for instance," Darcy continued, taking note of their obvious interest. She turned to show them the detailing on the back of the shirt. "Do you like it?"

Much to her surprise, Darcy's question was answered by a male voice. He gave her new shirt a resounding, "Yeah, baby, yeah!"

Darcy gasped. That bad Austin Powers imitation could only come from one person. . . .

Layne Haznoy!

She turned around slowly. Sure enough, there he was, standing in the doorway, wearing a poor-fitting

T-shirt bearing the words "I Am Special."

Well, there was an understatement. "Special" didn't *begin* to describe Layne! And *not* in a good way!

To make matters worse, Layne was carrying another creepy animal. This one also resembled a rat. Darcy frowned. What was it with this guy and rodents, anyway?

"Don't you think so, Mini Me?" Layne asked his ferret.

Darcy rolled her eyes. Just what she needed. Fashion commentary from a rat's cousin.

"Hello, Layne," Lindsay greeted him. "Nice ferret."

"There's something wrong with his tail," Layne explained.

Lindsay nodded. "Okay, Darcy, you hold him and I'll take a look."

Darcy sighed and took the ferret from Layne's arms. She placed him down on the counter.

"He smells funky," Kathi commented.

Darcy agreed. She held her arms out, trying to keep her distance from the smelly, struggling animal.

But Mini Me obviously liked to be held close. He wiggled around until he was free to climb up the front of Darcy's shirt. She looked down in horror as tiny rips began to appear in the silky lavender fabric.

"He's tearing my blouse!" she shouted out.

"Sorry," Layne apologized with a noncommittal shrug. "His claws are kinda sharp."

"That's okay," Darcy replied, barely masking her anger. "This blouse was several minutes old, anyway. I was getting tired of it."

Darcy's sarcasm was lost on Layne. "Too bad," he told her. "It was pretty."

Lindsay glanced up at Layne for a moment but said nothing. Instead, she gently ran her hand along Mini Me's back. "There's nothing wrong with his tail," she said finally.

"Are you sure?" Layne asked. "It was twitching before."

He looked down. Sure enough, the ferret's tail twitched back and forth quickly.

"What, like that?" Lindsay asked, pointing to the moving tail.

"Uh-huh."

Lindsay rolled her eyes. "It's *supposed* to do that."

"Oh, that's a relief," Layne replied. "Well, thanks." He reached into his pocket and pulled out his wallet. "I insist on paying this time." He lay a worn, folded piece of paper on the counter.

Lindsay picked up the paper and examined it

closely. "You're paying with a coupon?" she asked, surprised.

Layne smiled. "Yeah. It's good for one free soda at Stubby's Diner." He picked up his ferret and headed toward the door. "You take care now, ladies. Haznoy, out," he added in his very best Ryan Seacrest imitation. Which, not surprisingly, wasn't particularly good.

Darcy frowned as the door shut behind Layne and Mini Me. "He's very . . . colorful," she remarked, not knowing quite what to say about what she had just experienced.

"He's not colorful," Kathi differed. "He's in love." She paused for a minute and reconsidered that statement. "Okay, he's colorful and in love," she corrected herself. "He's obviously got a big crush on you."

Darcy looked at her strangely. "What? That's ridiculous."

Lindsay shook her head. "Hey, he's lived here all his life and he's always had a million pets. He's never brought them in here before," she told Darcy. "But now he's bringing them in and there's nothing even wrong with them."

"So?" Darcy asked.

"So the only new thing around here is you," Kathi pointed out.

"And the new shipment of dog toothpaste," Lindsay corrected her. "But I don't think that's what Layne's after."

Darcy refused to believe this. The idea that Layne might have a crush on her was just too . . . well . . . *icky* to consider. "That doesn't mean he's got a crush on me," she insisted.

"No," Lindsay agreed. "But this kind of does." She held up the coupon Layne had left behind. "He wrote you a poem."

Darcy grabbed the paper from Lindsay's hand and began to read what Layne had scribbled on it in his chicken-scratch handwriting.

From the day I saw Darcy
I knew from the start
That this was the girl
With the key to my heart.
—Haznoy, out!

Darcy sighed. There was no denying it now. "You're right, he's got a crush on me," she moaned.

Kathi and Lindsay began to giggle. Imagine someone like Layne going out with Darcy. It was too funny. But the look on Darcy's face stopped them cold. Obviously, she did not find this nearly as amusing as they did.

"I'm really gonna have nightmares tonight," Darcy sighed.

Chapter 11

Wild Wisdom . . . *A mole can dig a tunnel three hundred feet long in just one night.*

Darcy wasn't the only one to have an unwanted visitor complicating her life. That afternoon, Victoria discovered that the mole had once again dug his way into her garden, this time helping himself to some of her radishes.

This was war! That nasty mole was about to meet his match. Victoria had hired a professional trapper to catch the mole and take him someplace far from her ranch.

Of course, that job could become complicated if the mole invited some of his pals to dine on her vegetables with him. "How many moles do you suppose there are?" she asked Eli.

Eli thought for a moment. "Could be one. Could be more than one," he told her.

Victoria sighed. That wasn't particularly helpful.

"Well, I hope this animal trapper can catch them before they destroy my turnips."

Jack grimaced. Turnips? Ugh. "Yeah, that'd be a shame," he remarked sarcastically. Then he turned to Victoria. A smile came over his face as yet another brilliant plot came to mind. "You know, Mrs. Fields," he began. "This could be a great movie idea. You should call your Hollywood friends. Only instead of a regular mole, this could be a supergigantic flesh-eating mole that comes out of the toilet and eats you." He paused for a minute and smiled. "I'll let you be in it," he assured her.

Victoria sighed. "Really, Jack," she remarked sarcastically. "How kind."

Before Jack could reply, a dark, angry figure stomped across the ranch and into the garden where Victoria, Eli, and Jack stood.

The threesome stared at the newcomer, at first unable to determine if this long-haired stranger, dressed in a pair of dark jeans, an old weathered jacket, heavy cowboy boots, a well-worn cap, and large oversized mirrored sunglasses, was male or female. The name on the jacket read "RJ." That didn't even give them a clue. In fact, all they could tell at the moment was that this person was not someone to be messed with.

"You're the trapper?" Eli asked dubiously.

"No!" the visitor snapped back, in a voice that was obviously female.

Okay, so at least now they knew that much.

"I'm not the fer-cryin'-out-loud trapper!" she barked in Eli's face. "My dad's the trapper! But he don't waste his time catchin' no piddlin' little moles. So he sent me out here to give you tenderfoots a trap." RJ thrust a small metal box in Eli's direction.

Eli shuddered slightly at the sight of the box. He recognized it immediately as a humane trap. He'd just had a run-in with one of those—at Darcy's party. His foot was still smarting from being trapped in that thing. He wasn't anxious to handle another one.

But he was too afraid of RJ to say that. Gingerly, he took the box from her hands and held it.

"You need me to show you how to work it, you sorry little mouse-knocker?" she demanded.

"What do you think, Eli?" Victoria asked him kindly. "Can you handle it?"

Before Eli could even answer, RJ was in his face, barking orders like some sort of deranged drill sergeant. "You put some carrot or something in there, you lift that flap, and you set it where the mole is." She sneered at the farmhand's trembling lips. "You think you can manage that on your own, or do you need your momma to come hold your little baby-piddly hand?" she demanded, obviously pleased that she was scaring him.

"Um . . ." Eli gulped. He was too frightened to respond.

"All right then!" RJ snapped, obviously not about to accept any questioning of her orders. She turned on her thick black heels and stomped away from the garden. As she left, Victoria, Eli, and Jack could hear her muttering to herself. "Moles. 'Ooh, help us. We've got moles!' " she groused, obviously imitating her clients. "Of all the sorry little rat-spit, greenhorn wastes of space . . ."

For a minute, no one said anything. They just watched, and waited, until RJ was definitely out of earshot.

"She's scary," Eli said finally.

"I should say so," Victoria agreed.

But Jack didn't seem at all upset by RJ's visit. In fact, he seemed thrilled that she'd been there. She'd given him inspiration.

"There's a movie idea! *Trapped!*" he exclaimed as he spun around and pointed ominously at Eli. "She's coming after you."

Eli shuddered. Now *that* was a horror movie!

Darcy sat on a wooden bench at Creature Comforts and watched as Lindsay donned her surgical gloves and carefully threaded a needle.

"Okay, we're ready," Lindsay announced, holding the threaded needle high and carefully inspecting her patient. Then, finally satisfied that she knew exactly where to begin stitching, she carefully inserted the needle and pulled the thread through.

Darcy looked down and watched her, amazed at the tiny size of the stitch. There would barely be a scar. Her new blouse looked better already. Amazing! On top of everything else, Lindsay was a wonderful seamstress.

"Poor Layne," Darcy mused as Lindsay sewed. "I can't believe he has a crush on me." She paused for a moment, considering that statement. "Well, I *can* believe it," she corrected herself. "I mean, it's *me*. But still, I'm just not sure what to do about it."

Lindsay looked up from her stitching. "It's simple what you do," she told her pointedly. "You tell him the truth."

Darcy giggled. "Yeah, right. Come on, get serious." She looked into Lindsay's eyes. "Oh, you are serious."

"Lindsay might be right," Kathi interjected. "Just tell him you're not interested. Don't let it drag out."

Darcy shook her head vehemently. "That would hurt him too much," she insisted. "And let's not forget the *really* important thing—it would be *very* uncomfortable for me." She sat there for a moment, considering her options. But nothing immediately came to mind. This was very frustrating. When she'd lived in Malibu, she'd never had these kinds of problems. Not that there weren't any boys with crushes on her there. It was just that they didn't pose this kind of dilemma for her. Of course, back there she'd had experts that she could ask for really good advice.

"You know, my friend Shelby back home has dealt with stuff like this a couple of times. She's very popular with boys." Darcy leaned over and quietly confided in Lindsay and Kathi, "She developed early. I'll just do what she does."

"I bet this'll be good," Kathi said with excitement. Darcy's California friends always seemed intriguing to her.

From that moment on, Darcy felt more relaxed and upbeat. She knew that as soon as she figured out WWSD (What Would Shelby Do?) her problems would be solved.

❋ (**DARCY'S DISH**) ❋

SOS, Shelby . . .

I've got a total emergency here! You remember when I
wrote and told you my guy problem was that I didn't
have a guy? Well, I've got one now. Only he's not the
man of my dreams. He's more the man of my nightmares!

I know it's a totally scary thought, but there's a dweeb in
love with me. Actually, calling him a dweeb isn't really
fair . . . to the other dweebs out there. Layne is in a class
all by himself. Suffice it to say he has rodents for pets . . .
and not cute rodents like fuzzy bunnies and guinea pigs.
This guy has a bat and a ferret. And you should see the
clothes he wears. He's like a walking *Glamour* Don't!

Now you see why you gotta help me, Shel. I want to let
this guy down easy . . . while making it easy for me, too.
Any ideas?

Chapter 12

Wild Wisdom . . . *Cats purr at the same frequency as an idling diesel engine, about twenty-six cycles per second.*

By the next afternoon, Darcy had her answer from Shelby and was ready to put Operation Let Layne Down Easy into motion. And by the time he arrived at Creature Comforts—which she knew he would—she was ready for him.

"It's the Haz-nizzle in the Crizzle Hizzle," he announced himself, trying to sound like Snoop Dogg but coming across like plain old Layne.

"Okay, Layne, let me guess," Lindsay said, not even bothering to hide her exasperation. "Your cat grew a second head, but now it's gone away and the cat's fine."

"Naw," Layne said, seemingly unaware that Lindsay had been joking. "She's just a stray I found. She's acting kinda weird."

Lindsay smiled to herself. "Well, you ain't seen

nothing yet," she murmured. Then she turned toward the back room. "Darcy," she called out. "Layne's here."

Layne's eyes looked toward the office door with great anticipation. While he waited for Darcy's grand entrance, Lindsay took the stray from the carrier.

"Whoa!" she exclaimed. There wasn't much more to say. This was one ugly cat. Her fur was all mangy and matted, one of her eyes was swollen shut, and she really smelled.

But the cat had nothing on Darcy. When she emerged from the office, she looked every bit as mangy as the stray! She was a total mess—in a pair of frumpy overalls and an old worn-out shirt. Her hair, which was usually brushed and styled with great care, was tied up in pigtail-like bundles all around her head. She had smudges on her skin that resembled pimple cream. Worst of all, she was eating the most disgustingly stinky submarine sandwich ever.

"Whoa!" Layne exclaimed, sounding every bit as surprised by Darcy's appearance as Lindsay had been by the cat's.

Darcy smiled to herself. Obviously, her new look was having its desired effect on Layne. He looked absolutely repulsed. Now it was time to really make him sick.

"Heya, Laynie," she greeted him. She held up the putrid sub. "Just having an anchovy and onion sandwich. It's . . ."—she let out a huge belch— "mighty good." A pickle slipped out of the roll and fell to the floor. "Aw, shoot." Darcy frowned. She bent down, lifted the half-eaten pickle from the ground, and held it up to examine it in the light. After getting a good look, she shook her head. "Naw. Got a little too much dog hair on it." She held the pickle out in Layne's direction. "You want?"

Layne stared at her with bewilderment. "Um, no thanks," he replied.

Darcy put the pickle back in her pocket and stuck her finger up her nose. Then she lifted up her arm and took a good sniff of her pits. As she went through her total gross-out routine, Darcy was well aware of Layne's eyes. They hadn't left her, not once. Surely by now he was totally repulsed. She was certain he'd be out of there in no time.

At just that moment, Lindsay interrupted Darcy's performance. "Well, Layne," she said. "Turns out there actually *is* something going on with your cat."

Layne seemed genuinely surprised. "There is?"

"Yeah," Lindsay replied. "Besides being the ugliest cat I've ever seen, she's in estrus."

Darcy looked at her peculiarly. "What's that?" she asked.

"It's her season for mating," Lindsay explained. "All of her hormones are telling her to find a male cat, and it makes her restless."

The cat let out an ear-piercing meow, as if to agree with Lindsay's diagnosis.

"So what should I do?" Layne asked Lindsay.

"Get her spayed," Lindsay replied firmly. "It's the responsible thing to do—way too many unwanted cats and dogs get destroyed. We'll do the operation, but we can't start until she's out of estrus. Just leave her here and we'll do it when she's ready."

Layne looked from the scruffy cat to the shabby Darcy and back again. Then he quickly grabbed his pet carrier and headed for the door. "Oh, okay, well . . . thanks," he stammered nervously as he ran from the clinic.

As the door slammed shut behind Layne, Darcy turned to Lindsay and smiled triumphantly. "Aha! Mission accomplished," she declared victoriously. "He was so weirded out, he didn't even remember to say, 'Haznoy, out!' "

But Darcy's victory celebration was short-lived. Not a second later, she began to hear a rap beat coming from outside. A moment later, in walked Layne. This time, he was carrying a boom box instead of a pet carrier. And his fashion sense had changed, too. He was no longer just a geek—he was *street* geek. It was obvious he'd made an attempt to look like some sort of rap idol, what with his blue sweatband, red track jacket, and the largest, ugliest piece of fake bling Darcy had ever seen.

"Haznoy, in!" he announced himself as he set the blaring boom box on the counter. His arms and legs began moving in some sort of bizarre attempt at dancing. And that wasn't nearly as bad as his attempt at actual rapping:

"My name is Layne Thaddeus Haznoy.

You're a tasty lady, I'm a pretty boy.

There's a barn dance representin' Saturday night.

You're gonna be my date there, a'ight.

A'ight!

So I'll see you Saturday, girl,

We'll get to kickin' . . ."

"I've got to put ointment on your cat, she's lickin'," Lindsay interrupted him.

Layne stopped his boom box. That seemed as good an ending to his rap as any. He smiled broadly at Darcy. "So I'll see you Saturday. I'll pick you up around seven."

Darcy stared at him, not knowing what to say. This boy just couldn't take a hint. "But I . . ." she began.

"Haznoy, out!" Layne interrupted her, leaving the clinic before Darcy could finish her sentence. As he walked off, the girls could hear him singing to himself, "I've got a girlfriend! I've got a girlfriend!"

No sooner had Layne left than Kathi arrived at Creature Comforts. She was breathing heavily. Obviously, she'd run to the clinic.

"Did I miss anything? What happened?" she asked as she raced into the room.

Darcy didn't reply. She didn't have to. The sick expression on her face said it all.

Chapter 13

Wild Wisdom . . . *One mouse can eat eight pounds of food in a year.*

It was obvious to Darcy's friends that she had big problems. Darcy's mother, on the other hand, had only small problems . . . problems about the size of a garden mole.

Despite her best efforts, that cagey mole absolutely refused to be caught. At least not until he'd chomped on every vegetable in the garden.

But Victoria had news for him. That mole had met his match. One way or another, she was going to triumph over the carrot-chomping rodent—with Eli's help, of course.

"How's the mole trap working, Eli?" Victoria asked as she observed Eli placing the nozzle of a garden hose into the mole hole.

"Nothing so far," Eli replied. But he was far from

admitting defeat. "So I'm juicing it up. I'm putting the hose in this hole so the mole will get flushed out and come out of that hole over there." He pointed to a hole a few feet away, where he'd already placed the mole trap RJ had provided them with. "Then he'll run right into the trap. It's not like he'll see it, 'cause burrowing animals are pretty much blind in daylight."

Eli maneuvered the nozzle of the hose a few inches, until it was the perfect depth to reach the mole. Then he called over toward the side of the house, "Okay, Jack, hit it!"

Jack did as he was told. He turned the water up full blast and then waited to see what would happen.

Unfortunately, nothing did.

"Nothing's happening," Eli called over to Jack.

"It's on full blast," Jack assured him.

Eli reached down and yanked the hose from the ground. He held the nozzle faceup and peered inside. Maybe something was stuck in there.

But it was Victoria who spotted the problem. "Oh, your hose has a kink," she pointed out, reaching down to straighten out the bend in the garden hose.

Voom! A blast of water burst out of the hose, dousing Eli in the face. The force of all that water exploding out of the nozzle forced the hose from his hands. The green hose began shooting water straight up into the air, like a water-squirting serpent.

"Aw no," Eli moaned as he tried to leap out of the way of the cold, cascading water.

Victoria calmly raised her beige and blue Burberry umbrella to keep from getting wet. "I guess we'd better call and get another trap," she mused.

"No!" Eli insisted with uncharacteristic fervor. "That girl scares me. I'll figure out a way to catch this little guy on my own." He stopped for a minute, considering something. "Or her," he corrected himself. "I suppose it could be a her."

Unfortunately, by the next day Victoria still hadn't gotten rid of the mole that was ruining her garden. And Darcy hadn't managed to get rid of the boy who was ruining her life, either.

Darcy was becoming desperate. Shelby's plan had totally backfired. But now, Darcy had recruited the help of the big guns—her mother and a surprise guest star.

Lindsay stood behind the counter at Creature Comforts and studied Darcy's designer jeans and pretty pale blue T-shirt. "So, you're not in your hobo getup today."

"You're gonna tell Layne the truth?" Kathi asked.

The truth? Darcy shook her head emphatically. "No, no," she assured her. "I've come up with an even better plan."

Just then, the door swung open. Eli swaggered in, dressed in a surprisingly hip outfit—button-down shirt, designer jeans, and cowboy boots.

"Where's my darling Darcy?" he asked in an extremely proprietary voice. "I've been working all day and I want to see my woman. I've been working on my dance moves. . . ." He stopped talking long enough to do a few spins. They were pretty impressive, considering this was *Eli* doing the dancing. He'd obviously had a few lessons in the weeks since the pirate party.

Kathi and Lindsay stared at Eli. They weren't sure which was more shocking, the fact that he'd actually managed to spin around without falling on his face, or the fact that he'd just called Darcy his woman.

"That was really good, Eli," Darcy complimented him. "But Layne's not here yet, so you can relax."

Lindsay and Kathi exchanged looks. That explained it—Darcy had recruited Eli to help her get rid of Layne.

"Good," Eli replied as he sunk into a chair beside an old man who was sleeping on a bench in the corner of the room. He removed a bag of crackers from his jacket pocket and began munching on them, stopping only once in a while to feed a cracker crumb to a tiny mouse who had made a place for himself in the old man's hat.

"This is not a better plan, Darcy," Lindsay differed. "Just tell Layne the truth."

Darcy rolled her eyes. Why was Lindsay so insistent about this truth thing? "In a way, I'm telling him the truth," she said, trying to placate her.

"By pretending Eli's your boyfriend?" Kathi wondered out loud. "Isn't that kind of using him?"

"Oh, I'm cool with it," Eli assured her. "I've never dated a movie star's daughter."

"But you're *not* dating," Kathi pointed out. "It's fake."

Eli shrugged. "Hey, it's the closest I've ever gotten," he replied.

Darcy studied Eli carefully. He cleaned up really nicely. But would Layne believe that Darcy would date Eli? She thought about that for a minute. Sure he would, she decided. After all, Layne believed Darcy would date *him*. And Layne was much less her type.

Just then, the boy in question burst through the door of Creature Comforts with a huge box in his hand. "Hey, ladies," Layne greeted everyone in a voice that

was an obvious attempt—and failure—at sounding
suave. "I arrive from Middle Earth bearing the gifts
of the elves."

Darcy stared at him, completely dumbstruck. She
hadn't thought anything could be worse than Layne's
obsession with Austin Powers. But this *Lord of the
Rings* thing was even more ridiculous.

Before Layne could magically become Frodo
before their eyes, the phone rang. Kathi was the first
to reach it. "Creature Comforts, Kathi speaking. I
don't work here."

Luckily, it wasn't a customer on the other end. It
was Victoria. She could no longer sit at home without
hearing what was happening at the clinic. "How's it
going so far?" she asked Kathi anxiously. "Eli was
adorable in rehearsals."

"Layne just arrived from Middle Earth, bearing
gifts from the elves," Kathi informed her.

"Brilliant," Victoria exclaimed. "Keep me posted."

Kathi stared incredulously into the receiver. She
couldn't believe what she'd just heard. Obviously,
Darcy had filled her mom in on the whole Layne
deal, and Victoria had helped create the plan to make
Eli seem like Darcy's boyfriend. Boy, Hollywood
families sure were different. No mom in Bailey would

ever do that!

While Kathi marveled over how cool Victoria was, Darcy watched with amazement as Layne opened the box and pulled out a red-and-white checked . . . *something*.

"What . . . what is it?" Darcy asked, staring at the piece of garish gingham fabric.

"It's a dress for you to wear to the dance," Layne told her proudly.

"Really?" Lindsay asked. "Because it looks like a tablecloth."

Layne ignored Lindsay completely but smiled kindly at Darcy. "I felt sorry for you 'cause you looked kind of raggedy the other day. It's about time you let your sugar start dressing you nice."

Darcy gulped. If Layne was her sugar, she was definitely swearing off carbs for a while! And as for this dress . . . she held it up against her. There was no way she was going to be seen in a red-and-white checked dress with puffy sleeves and frilly skirt. It looked like something square dancers wore. And Darcy was anything but square!

This had to stop. And now! It was time to put her Eli plan into action. "Oh yeah . . . about that," she began. "See, the thing is, Layne, I already have a boyfriend." She turned toward the chair, where Eli was busy chowing down on his crackers. "Don't I, sweetheart?"

Eli pulled another cracker from the bag, examined it, and popped it into his mouth. He didn't seem to hear Darcy at all.

"Honey?" Darcy said, trying to get Eli's attention. But Eli was completely focused on his cracker. "ELI!" Darcy shouted out finally.

That last one startled him right into action. "Oh yeah. Darcy's my woman," he said. Then, as if to prove it, he rolled up his shirtsleeve to reveal something written there. "Milk, bread, cereal, eggs . . ." he began. Oops. "Wrong arm," he corrected himself. "That's my shopping list. Quickly, he rolled up the other sleeve to reveal a big heart with the name "Darcy" in the center. "See, it says so right here. Our love is a love for the ages, written in the annals of time . . . in washable marker." Eli smiled triumphantly, obviously pleased that he had gotten his lines right.

But Layne was unimpressed. "Sorry, pal, but things change," he said, staring Eli straight in the eye. "Darcy's going to the dance with me. So I guess she's not with you."

"No, Layne," Darcy interrupted.

But Layne was determined to set the record straight. "Don't get upset, Boo. I can handle this," he assured Darcy. She grimaced at the sound of a pet name coming from Layne's lips, but he didn't seem to notice. Instead, he focused his attention on Eli. "You just have to accept it. She's pitched her tent in the Layne National Forest."

Darcy looked at him strangely. *The what?*

"Tell you what," Layne continued, "just so there's no hard feelings, I'll buy you a sandwich."

That was all it took. "All right!" Eli exclaimed as he headed for the door.

Darcy frowned. Obviously, the adage was true— the way to a man's heart was through his stomach. Eli was going where the eats were.

"Gotta jet, doll," Layne told Darcy. "Can't wait to see you in that dress."

As if that is ever going to happen! Darcy looked helplessly in Lindsay's direction. But even Lindsay couldn't get her out of this jam.

As the boys left the clinic, Darcy sighed. "Thanks for not saying 'I told you so,' " she told Lindsay.

"I haven't said it—yet," Lindsay corrected her. Then she added, "I told you so."

Darcy scowled. She knew that was coming.

"This has to stop," Lindsay continued sternly. "He's disrupting the clinic, he's wasting my time . . ."

"He's bringing *me* clothes a clown wouldn't be caught dead in," Darcy reminded her.

"So tell him the truth," Lindsay insisted. "Because if you don't, I will," she warned.

Darcy gulped. Lindsay wasn't kidding.

Darcy looked down at the frilly red-and-white checked hoedown getup Layne had given her to wear on Saturday night. That settled it. She was going to have to give Layne the old heave-ho (in a nice way, of course) . . . and fast! Otherwise, she was going to actually have to wear the thing! A boy crisis was one thing, but a fashion crisis was out of the question!

Chapter 14

Wild Wisdom . . . *Moles have about twice as much blood as other small mammals, which allows them to breathe better underground.*

Darcy may not have liked the idea of a pest like Layne sticking to her like glue, but Victoria was quite fond of the idea. Of course in her case, she was just hoping glue would be a solution to the rodent problem in her garden. To that end, she'd gone out and bought some specially made sticky-paper glue traps. Her plan was to lay them all over the garden so that the mole had to land on at least one. He wouldn't be able to sneak around them. She smiled proudly at her own ingenuity. Now this would get that sneaky mole!

But Eli wasn't nearly as enthusiastic as Victoria was about the new plan. In fact, later that afternoon as he reported for work at the ranch, he totally freaked out when he saw Victoria preparing to lay her traps. "You're not using sticky paper, are you, Mrs. Fields?"

"Well, yes," Victoria replied, obviously unaware of any trouble that might cause. "This way, when the mole comes out, he'll stick to it, and we can let him go somewhere else."

As usual, Jack had been trailing Victoria, hoping for an entry into the Hollywood scene. His face brightened. This was it! He had an idea that he was certain Victoria would go for. "That would make a good superhero," he told her excitedly. "Sticky Man. When evildoers try to get away with something, they just stick to him."

Victoria sighed and rolled her eyes slightly. "I'll get Hollywood on the phone," she murmured sarcastically. Then she thought for a moment. "Although they've done much worse . . ." she admitted.

Before Jack could manage to come up with an entire movie plot, Darcy approached the garden. In her hands was a pet carrier. There was no reason for Victoria, Eli, or Jack to ask what kind of creature was inside—the constant whine of meowing gave it away. Darcy had brought home a cat. And not just any cat. She'd brought home Layne's stray—the one who was most definitely in heat.

"*MEEEEOOOOOWWWWWW!*" As the cat let out another painful cry, Darcy frowned. *Life in the country is just filled with glamour*, she thought ruefully.

"Heya, Darcy," Eli called out to her.

But Darcy wasn't about to be all chummy with him. "I don't want to talk to you," she snapped. "He sold me out for a sandwich," she explained in response to her mother's confused look.

"He got me potato salad, too," Eli corrected her. "He's not a bad guy."

But Darcy wasn't convinced. "Now I'm stuck with Layne's mangy cat," she continued. "We ran out of kennel space at the clinic, so I have to keep her for a few days." She did not sound happy about it.

Just then, the cat let out a painful yelp. Apparently, *she* wasn't too crazy about the idea, either.

As Darcy left to bring the cat into the house, Eli turned his attention back to the mole trap. "I'm afraid the sticky paper will hurt the mole, Mrs. Fields," he told her. "I've got a better idea. Trust me." He reached down and picked up a glue trap.

Bad move. After all, sticky paper doesn't know the difference between a mole and someone's hand. Eli was stuck. He yanked and yanked, but that sticky paper remained stuck. And that wasn't all. There was a piece on his shoe, too. He reached down with his free hand to yank the sticky paper off his heel . . . and somehow managed to get that hand stuck to his foot.

Eli sat down and tried to wrench his hand free from his shoe. Unfortunately, he sat right on another piece of sticky paper. Now he was getting frustrated. He put his hand to his face, forgetting about the sticky paper on his palm. His hand attached itself to his face. Now Eli was stuck from top to bottom . . . literally. As he shook his head, trying to free his cheek from his hand, he toppled over into a pile of sticky paper. He rolled over, trying to get up, but somehow he managed to fall into a pile of hay. Suddenly, Eli looked remarkably like a scarecrow.

"Okay, Eli, I guess you've earned my trust," Victoria said, trying hard not to make the teen feel any worse by laughing. But it was no use. This was pretty incredible—even for Eli. "Hang on," she shouted as she scampered toward the house. "I've just got to get my camera."

It took a long while, but Eli eventually managed to pick the straw off his body and free himself from the maze of sticky paper he'd gotten himself trapped in. And he emerged from his glue-trap battle more determined than ever to capture that mole, his way. It was a matter of honor.

Besides, he had a plan—one that would necessitate

his unique bird-calling talent. Victoria was new in town, so she had no idea that Eli was a master of birdcalls. But she was about to find out. As Eli stood above the mole hole with a large net in hand, he revealed his plan to Victoria and Jack. "Hawks are moles' natural enemies," he explained. "I'm really good at hawk calls, so I'll just imitate a hawk near this hole, the mole will get scared, and he'll come out of that hole." He pointed toward a second hole, several feet away. "Then you get him with the net, Mrs. Fields," he continued, handing Victoria the net.

Victoria and Jack exchanged glances. Victoria was dubious, but Jack was kind of impressed. "It could work," he told her.

That was enough to convince Victoria. She walked over and planted herself at the second hole, net at the ready.

"SCREEECH!" Eli let out an ear-piercing imitation of a hawk. *"SCREEECH!"*

"He's actually pretty convincing," Victoria noted.

Jack looked up. "Guess so," he agreed, pointing up to the sky. The mother hawk whose nest was in Victoria's tree had taken off in flight. As the magnificent bird swooped down and headed toward Eli, the farmhand took off and tried to get out of her way.

Unfortunately, he tripped over the net Victoria had been holding. *Boom!* He landed hard on the ground. The mother hawk dove right for him.

"I guess Eli's good at mating calls," Victoria remarked with a chuckle.

Jack laughed along with her. "I don't know why I keep trying to think of movie ideas," he joked. "I should just point a camera at Eli."

Victoria and Jack may have gotten a good laugh at Eli's expense, but Darcy was definitely not in a laughing mood. In fact, this whole Layne mess was getting her down in a big way. And with Lindsay doing the whole I-told-you-so thing, and Kathi basically insisting that she tell Layne the truth, Darcy didn't feel there was anyone in all of Bailey who understood her dilemma.

Good thing she still had friends back in Malibu who were on her wavelength. And all she needed to reach them was her laptop. Sending out a blog to her peeps would surely make her feel better. So she pulled her laptop up on her bed and began sending out the 411 on her situation.

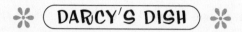

✳ (DARCY'S DISH) ✳

Hey, my people. Remember that weird guy I told you all about? I cannot get rid of him. I even tried Shelby's gross-out technique, and he still likes me! How annoying is that?

"Eeyow!"

Before Darcy could finish her blog update, Layne's cat let out another penetrating yowl. Darcy looked over in her direction and scowled. "Speaking of annoying," she told the cat, "you're getting more annoying than your owner."

"Eeyow!" The cat howled again.

Darcy reached down and opened the front of the cat carrier. "If I let you out of your carrier, will you be quiet for a while? All the doors and windows are shut, so you can't go outdoors," she explained to the wild cat. "But you can have the run of the house. There's some kibble down there that you can finish."

But surprisingly, it wasn't freedom the mangy feline was after. She just wanted a little love. And she instinctively knew how to get it. She leaped gracefully onto the bed and cuddled in Darcy's lap.

"Oh, hi," Darcy welcomed the cat with a new warmth in her voice. "How are you?" As if to answer her, the cat rubbed up against Darcy's shoulder and purred contentedly. Darcy reached over and petted the cat's soft fur. Within moments, the cat was asleep, breathing softly in Darcy's lap.

Darcy sat there for a moment, watching as the cat's small body moved up and down with each breath. There was something incredibly calming and therapeutic about seeing this little creature sleep so soundly. It really made her think.

Darcy reached over to her laptop, moving ever so gently so she wouldn't wake the cat. She had something she wanted to add to her post.

❀ (DARCY'S DISH) ❀

You know what, people? There are a lot of weird, annoying animals in the world. But I guess they all need affection. I suppose everybody's just looking for someone to be with.

❀   ❀   ❀   ❀   ❀   ❀

Darcy studied the post for a minute. When she was satisfied that she'd said all she needed to, she pressed Send. Then she closed the laptop, turned off

the lamp beside her bed, and lay down beside the cat. There was a contented smile on Darcy's face. It would be nice to cuddle with the soft warm creature all night.

"EEEEYOWWW!"

Darcy leaped up, shocked by the cat's sudden yelp.

Okay, so maybe a night with this cat wasn't going to be so great after all!

Chapter 15

Wild Wisdom . . . *A snake's heart can slide one to one and a half times its length from its normal position to allow for the passage of swallowed prey.*

When Victoria awoke the next morning and walked outside, she was shocked by what had happened to her garden. The entire area had been blanketed with old-fashioned, spring-loaded rat traps. They were set up like lethal dominoes near the mole hole.

Victoria sighed heavily. There was only one person who could be responsible for this. JACK!

Sure enough, the little guy was in the middle of the garden dolloping spoonfuls of peanut butter from a large bowl onto the traps. He seemed incredibly proud of himself. He was going to be the one to catch the mole. He'd be the anti-mole superhero!

But hero? Victoria certainly didn't share that opinion. She didn't want the mole in her garden, but she didn't want him to be sentenced to death for eating a few carrots, either. "Isn't this a little cruel, Jack?" she asked him.

"Nothing else is working," Jack insisted. "It's time to finish this." He gave Victoria a huge smile. "You can reward me later."

Just then, Eli walked up toward the house. When he saw the traps, he became furious. "Hey, what are you doing?" he demanded.

"Don't worry, Eli," Victoria calmed him down. "We both know Jack's going to wind up in those traps."

Eli shook his head. "Well, I'm not taking any chances," he declared as he took the apple he was holding and tossed it onto the nearest trap. Sure enough, the trap snapped shut. Then the force of the first trap snapping set the second trap into motion. Before long, the traps were snapping down like dominoes.

"Aaagh!" Jack shouted as one rat trap snapped shut close to his feet. He leaped out of the way. Another trap shut. Then another. And another. He hopped around, trying to avoid being caught in his own traps. But he lost his footing and . . . *splat*! Jack landed face-first in the bowl of peanut butter.

Now it was Eli's turn to laugh. Seeing Jack with a

face of peanut butter was payback for the satay situation at Darcy's party, the photos of him wrapped in sticky tape, and all of the other times Jack had laughed at Eli's expense. "Ha!" Eli chuckled. "Somebody else falling down for a change!"

Famous last words.

SNAP! Just as Eli was laughing at Jack, he got caught in a trap, too!

"OW!!!!!" the furious farmhand shouted. He lifted his leg and shook his foot hard, trying to release the trap. But the force of his shaking leg sent him spiraling backward. He landed in a pile of unused traps.

Victoria shook her head as she watched both Jack and Eli squirming around on the ground. "And the balance of nature has been restored," she noted with a grin as she headed back into the house to make a phone call. Jack had been right about one thing: It was time to finish this.

About an hour later, RJ reappeared at the ranch. If possible, she seemed even more ornery than the last time. She stomped up to the front porch where Victoria was sipping a mug of coffee and where Darcy and Eli were sort of staring at each other. It was too early in the morning for Darcy to make conversation.

In fact, she was still in her pajamas. From the look on RJ's face, Darcy could tell she disapproved of that. Not that RJ could talk about fashion. Darcy wasn't exactly into her cowboy-military ensemble, either.

"I can't believe you little mouse-knockin' greenhorns. I gotta waste my fer-crying-out-loud morning comin' out here because you're all so piddly and no-account you can't catch one sorry little mole?" she demanded. "Where's his hole?"

Eli gulped and pointed toward the garden. "He's no ordinary mole," he insisted to RJ as she stomped off in the direction of the mole hole. "He's obviously crafty, and much smarter than . . ."

Eli never got a chance to finish his sentence. Within seconds, RJ was back, holding the tiny mole in a cage. "Got him," she declared triumphantly. She held the little guy up so she could get a good look at him. "Cute little guy," she mused. "Think I'll keep him as a pet."

Darcy frowned. "Kind of a weird animal to have for a pet," she said.

RJ snickered. "I got lots of weird pets," she informed Darcy. "I like 'em weird. I got a squirrel without a tail, I got a woodpecker, I got a donkey that thinks I'm its momma."

Eli shot her a look. It was obvious he didn't find that too hard to believe.

Darcy was looking at RJ, too. But she had something completely different on her mind. . . .

Whatever Darcy was up to, it was taking her a long time. In fact, she was late to work that afternoon. That annoyed Lindsay on two levels. For one thing, she hated it when Darcy pulled her irresponsible Malibu act. For another, Darcy's absence meant Lindsay had to deal with Layne's latest visit. This time, he arrived with a long green snake in hand.

"I can save you some time, Layne," Lindsay huffed. "Your snake's fine, and Darcy's not here yet."

Layne didn't seem upset that Darcy hadn't arrived. In fact, Darcy not being there provided him with an excellent opportunity to get some info about her.

"Maybe you can tell me what her favorite flower is," Layne suggested to Lindsay. "I want to get her a corsage to go with her dress."

"I don't know what her favorite flower is," Lindsay replied.

"Is it tulips?" Layne continued, badgering her. "I bet it's tulips."

Lindsay was pretty certain Darcy wouldn't be caught dead in a corsage made of big tulips. She was also definitely certain that she was sick of having Layne hang out at Creature Comforts. Unable to contain her anger any longer, she shouted out, "Layne, I DON'T KNOW!"

It should have been impossible for anyone not to hear the furor in Lindsay's tone, but somehow Layne managed to miss it. He pointed his snake's head right at Lindsay. "Maybe it's bird-of-paradise . . ." he continued.

"LAYNE!" Lindsay shouted out angrily. She stared at him. Enough was enough. This whole Layne drama was going to have to come to an end. And it was going to happen now. "Y'know what?" she continued. "I didn't want to be the one to tell you this, but Darcy's not interested in you. She doesn't like you in that way."

Layne gasped and stood there for a minute, trying to process what Lindsay had just told him. "What? . . . what do you mean?"

Lindsay's frustration gave way to pity. Layne looked like a hurt puppy, and Lindsay wasn't one to kick a dog. "I mean, she doesn't want to go to the dance with you," she explained, her voice taking on a more gentle cadence. "She was afraid to tell you because she thought you'd be hurt."

Layne grabbed his stomach and bent over. He looked as though he'd been punched. He opened his mouth and emitted a low, guttural, painful moan— more pitiful than any sound his stray cat had made. It was a cry of sheer pain and distress, and it cut Lindsay right to her soul.

"I guess maybe she was right," Lindsay murmured quietly, finding that hard to believe, and yet knowing that it was probably true. Darcy did know more about boy-girl, social kinds of stuff.

Lindsay gave Layne a pitying smile and tried her best to smooth things over a little bit. "Look, Layne, don't be . . ." she began. She searched her mind for some comforting words that might let him see this was all for the best, but words just didn't come to her. So she awkwardly reached over and patted him gently on the arm. That was all the encouragement he needed. Layne suddenly pulled Lindsay close and buried his pained face in her shoulder.

Lindsay shuddered slightly. This was more than she had bargained for. When Darcy got to work, Lindsay was going to get her for leaving her with this. In fact . . .

At just that moment, the door burst open and

Darcy strolled inside. "Oh, good Layne, you're here," she greeted him in a light, breezy voice.

But Layne was in no mood for a happy Darcy. He knew the truth now, and it stung. "Yeah, so?" he replied.

Darcy grinned brightly. "So . . ." she began, in a voice filled with promise. Then she stepped aside and allowed a girl with dark reddish-brown hair to enter. The girl was wearing the red-and-white checked dress Layne had given Darcy. And she actually seemed to enjoy wearing it.

"Look, it's RJ, the trapper's daughter!" Darcy introduced her excitedly. Layne had probably met RJ around town at some point, seeing as they were both Bailey natives, but Darcy definitely thought a new introduction was necessary. After all, there was no way Layne would have recognized RJ. She looked completely different. Thanks to Darcy's skill with hair and makeup, RJ looked . . . well . . . she looked like a girl!

"Hi," Layne greeted her noncommittally.

"I hope you don't mind that I gave her the dress," Darcy told him. "It goes so well with her hair."

RJ smiled shyly. "My dad says I look like Cameron Diaz."

Everyone in the room stared at her. RJ certainly

looked a lot better now that her hair was combed and she was out of her armylike uniform. But *Cameron Diaz* . . .

Only Layne seemed to see that one. "Say, yeah, you kind of do," he told her.

"Hey, that's a righteous rat snake you got there," RJ said, noticing the long sinuous creature in Layne's hands.

"Oh, thanks!" Layne replied proudly.

"I got me one just like it," RJ boasted. "Caught it in a tree stump on old Ward Road."

"Really?" Layne asked with a new sense of interest in his voice. "I found a hurt opossum out there once. Named it Frodo."

"Frodo. That's a stinkin' cute name," RJ complimented him.

Darcy smiled. This wasn't exactly the kind of flirtatious repartee she was used to. And yet, it seemed to be working.

"We should go out to Ward Road sometime, see what's out there," Layne suggested.

RJ shrugged. "Why not now?"

Layne grinned broadly. Obviously, this fascinating creature in the red-and-white gingham square-dancing dress had gotten under his skin. "Great!" he exclaimed. He headed toward the door with RJ beside him.

"Layne," Darcy called out to him. "Before you go, I have to be honest with you. I didn't . . ."

But Layne didn't let her finish. "Whoa, Darcy, I'm sorry, but you and I are . . . well . . . *no mas*. Which is Spanish for *sayonara*," Layne interrupted with his usual slightly bizarre bravado. "I'm sure you'll be able to move on."

Darcy and Lindsay watched in amazement as the happy couple left the animal clinic. For a moment, neither of them spoke. Then finally, Lindsay remarked, "I think you just got dumped."

"I think I did," Darcy agreed quietly. Then a broad grin spread across her face. "Yes!" she shouted as she dropped to one knee and victoriously pumped the air with her fist.

As Darcy got back up, Lindsay looked her straight in the eye. "Y'know, you were kinda right that being brutally honest could be, well . . . brutal."

Darcy was definitely taken aback. Partly because Lindsay hardly ever admitted Darcy was right. And partly because Darcy had been thinking that *Lindsay* was right all along.

"Yeah, but you were right that if I'd been up-front

with him, we wouldn't have had to go through all this," Darcy admitted.

Lindsay thought for a moment. "I guess there aren't any easy answers for this stuff," she said finally.

"No. But at least *Layne's* got a date for the dance," Darcy pointed out. Whereas she and Lindsay were going to have to go dateless. Unless . . .

Darcy got that smile on her face—the one she always got when an idea came to her.

Surprisingly, the same smile was mirrored on Lindsay's face. The girls knew exactly who to call for just this kind of emergency!

"ELI!" they yelled together as they ran for the door.

The night after the dance, Darcy sat down in front of her laptop and sent a blog to her pals back in Malibu.

 **DARCY'S DISH**

Hey, people!

Just got back from a dance at my new high school. It wasn't at all like the ones we're used to. No Top 40 band, no caviar appetizers, and no designer dresses. But it did have one thing in common with the dances I knew back home—it was impossible to figure out what the boys wanted. They went to the dance, sure. But they didn't necessarily dance. (Sound familiar?) And the ones who did dance . . . well . . . I wish I could describe the way my friend Eli looks when he's making his moves, but it sort of defies words.

Anyhow, I had a blast, 'cuz I spent the night rockin' out with my pals Lindsay and Kathi. (Yeah, check it out, Lindsay went to a dance, cut loose, and had fun! I am definitely making progress here!) We didn't need any dates. Sometimes girls can just have fun with one another. You know, it's a chick thing!

Behind the Scenes
at
Darcy's Wild Life

LIFE as Darcy Fields knows it comes to an end when her movie-star mom decides the family needs a simpler life and moves them to a working rural farm. But Darcy's new "wild life" is filled with new friends, new animals, and new adventures! Here's a look at the cast and characters of your favorite TV and book series:

DARCY FIELDS is a good-hearted teenaged girl raised with every imaginable luxury in Malibu and Beverly Hills, California. The daughter of a movie star, she's accustomed to private jets and movie premieres, so she is staggered to find herself working at a veterinary clinic and tending to animals in the middle of nowhere. Luckily, her irrepressible good nature and basic affection for people in general helps her find reserves of self-reliance and resourcefulness she never knew she possessed.

VICTORIA FIELDS is an eccentric British movie star who adores her daughter, Darcy. Which explains why Victoria decided to quit showbiz and move Darcy to a remote ranch so Darcy could have a "normal" upbringing, far from the glamour and glitz of Hollywood. Generous, warm, and extravagant, Victoria enjoys whatever she is doing and throws herself into it 100 percent.

LINDSAY ADAMS is a levelheaded small-town girl in her early teens who initially has little patience for Darcy's Hollywood glamour when Darcy starts working at Creature Comforts. Lindsay is a bit skeptical of people in general, and tends to find animals less complicated and more reliable. Once Darcy proves herself to Lindsay, however, the two girls become loyal friends and allies.

JACK ADAMS is a ten-year-old schemer who keeps himself—and everyone else—busy with the crazy plans he constantly has up his sleeve. Quick-witted and energetic, Lindsay's little brother may be pint-sized, but his dreams are always larger than life.

DR. KEVIN ADAMS is a small-town veterinarian, father of Lindsay and Jack, and Darcy's new boss at Creature Comforts. Dr. Adams is confident and self-assured when treating animals, but his veterinary skills seem to use up most of his available powers of concentration. In other areas of his life, Kevin can be vague and sometimes a little clueless, but his endless friendliness and curiosity about people make Dr. Adams content in any situation.

ELI is a local ranch kid with an encyclopedic knowledge of local animals and their habitat. The breadth of his knowledge is matched by the depth of his clumsiness, and while he's always ready to pitch in and help out with chores, the likely outcome of his efforts will be light to moderate bumps and bruises. Meet Eli and you'll buy stock in the Ace bandage company.

KATHI GIRALDI is a local teenager with a warm heart and a huge desire to know anything and everything about Hollywood. Kathi is beside herself when "it" girl Darcy moves to town, and she idolizes Darcy as she would a big sister.

And enjoy this sneak peek at Darcy's continuing
online blog, Darcy's Blog! Darcy's blog
keeps her friends near and far up to date
with her latest adventures.

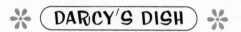

❋ (DARCY'S DISH) *❋*

4:10 PM—Hey, my people, I'm here to report on a
terrifying encounter with an adorable, death-dealing
puppy. I was petting this really cute little guy at
Creature Comforts, and he bit me right on my hand.
I'm sure he didn't mean anything personal by it—my
hand happened to be covered with hamburger at the
time, and he was just chowing down. But the thing is,
Lindsay said that he could have maybe had rabies,
which would mean I would have had to have all kinds
of painful rabies shots, and anyone who knows me
knows that feeling pain is on my list of least favorite
things.

Luckily, he was fine, but now Lindsay wants me to
read up on all sorts of veterinary stuff, since I work at
an animal clinic and everything. I guess that makes
sense, but the more time I spend reading about animal diseases, the less time I have to read about really
important stuff, like Halle Berry's beauty tips. Man,
the sacrifices I make...

6:45 PM—AAAGGGHHHHHHHH! Let me repeat that—
AAAGGGHHHHHHHH!

My people, you're not gonna believe all the gross things
that can happen to animals. I'm talkin' way worse than
when my friend Ashlee Cho's cat coughed up a hairball
in the middle of her makeover party.

I've been reading these veterinary books and it turns
out there's all kinds of scary diseases you can get from
animals, too, like Lyme Disease and Mad Cow Disease—
there are more -itises and -opathies and -phomas than
there are Wayans Brothers, and who knows how many
Wayans Brothers there are?

To tell you the truth, it creeps me out a little.

1:05 AM—Okay, I guess it creeps me out more than a
little. It's more like I'm freaked out so much that now
I'm the Mayor of Freak-Out Land.

Part of it is Eli's fault—he keeps telling me about how
wild animals can rip buildings apart and eat everybody
in the world without even breaking a sweat, and how
there are snakes so poisonous that your head would

explode from the pain if they ever even sneezed on you. And part of it's my mom's fault, because she wants to go camping. That's right—camping. Not in a hotel where they have fluffy towels and room service and masseuses, but in a tent, where they have dirt and bugs and animals that think you're breakfast.

I don't think I want to go camping...

11:00 AM—My mom thinks I should help Jack make some crazy video about animals, that he thinks he can sell to show to other animals. (Jack can be kind of weird sometimes, but I think you already knew that.) My mom thinks if I get out around animals, I might not be so freaked out about them. To me, that's kind of like telling Harry Potter that if he hung around more with Voldemort that they might turn out to be buds, but I guess I'll give it a try.

5:00 PM—So, my people, I took my life in my hands and helped Jack with his "chick flick." I swear, every single animal on the ranch is out to get me.

I still don't want to go camping. In fact, now I don't even want to go outside.

12:35 PM—Hola, folks. Here's a problem with being scared to death of animals—it makes it kind of impossible to work at a veterinary clinic. So I had to quit.

Bummer, huh?

3:00 PM—My people, I'm here to report that living indoors 24/7 isn't so bad. You catch up on your snacking, with no danger of being snacked upon yourself.

And when you spend as much time as I do just staring at the walls, you come up with lots of new ways to say "beige." For instance: "Off-white." "Sand." "Wall-colored." See how fun?

3:05 PM—Okay, the truth is that staying inside all the time is a big, fat, boring drag. But what can I do? If I go outside, I'll get eaten by a goose or a walrus or something.

10:30 PM—Okay, my people, I'm here to tell you about Darcy's Miracle Remedy. If you're ever feeling kind of down, or like you can't get a handle on stuff, here's what you do: You help a horse give birth.

Okay, I know that might not be a handy fix for everybody, 'cause you can't always count on having a pregnant horse nearby at the exact right time, but it worked for me.

Kevin Adams needed me to help him deliver a baby horse tonight, and it was so cool. (It was also a little on the slimy side, to tell you the truth, but mostly it was cool.) And how could something as cute as a baby horse want to eat me? It couldn't, that's how. And if baby horses don't want to eat me, then maybe not every other animal out there wants to eat me, either. And that means that I can go outside again, and go work at Creature Comforts again, and that's the beauty of Darcy's Miracle Remedy.

But I'm still going to keep my eye on geese. Those things bite.

(catch more Darcy's Dish on www.discoverykids.com)

Q & A WITH STAN ROGOW, EXECUTIVE PRODUCER FOR *DARCY'S WILD LIFE*

What was the inspiration for *Darcy's Wild Life*?
The inspiration was really teen literature. There is a history of books about girls and horses and the emotional connection between them. That, in its most elemental form, parallels the emotional growth that kids go through during the teen or tween years, which is what this series is all about.

What defines Darcy's character?
The most interesting part of Darcy's character is that not much can stop her. When confronted with a problem, she says, "It's okay. How will I get to the other side of this?" She's a strong spirit and unrelentingly optimistic and she provides kids with the inspiration for positively dealing with their circumstances.

Darcy embraces this new lifestyle rather quickly. Is that something that would happen in real life?
I think that's Darcy. Her adaptation is ongoing but her take on the situation is: "Here's what I got served up in life, and I am going to make it work."

What were you looking for when you cast the character of Darcy?

We were looking for somebody who embodies Darcy's elemental goodness and her fundamental strengths. What we found in Sara Paxton is an inherent wide-eyed optimism that is exactly right for this role.

What are some of the important life lessons that Darcy will learn throughout the series?

The large life lessons that all kids watching the show will learn is an acceptance of who they are. Who you are is fundamentally okay . . . even if you are different. None of these characters are exactly perfect, but somewhere in the mix of all of them, hopefully, there is some pretty interesting stuff.